SPIRIT CHASER

JaLynn

I know that
you will know

Paul

12-17-17

SPIRIT CHASER

Paul McElroy

Treasure Coast Mysteries, Inc.
43 Kindred Street
Stuart, FL. 34994

www.TreasureCoastMysteries.com

Printed in United States of America

Publication date June 2005
1   3   5   7   9   1 0   8   6   4   2
Copyright © 2005 by Paul E. McElroy
All rights reserved.

Publisher
Treasure Coast Mysteries, Inc.
43 Kindred Street
Stuart, FL 34994
772-288-1066

LIBRARY OF CONGRESS CATALOGING-IN-PUBLICATION DATA:
McElroy, Paul E.
SPIRIT CHASER by Paul E. McElroy
144 Pages   6" x   9"
Trade paperback

ISBN 0-9715136-4-3

1.   Emma, the kindred spirit of a deceased woman trapped in a hospital, assists
terminal patients to make peace with their family before they pass – Fiction.
2. Mystery – Florida - Fiction
3. Florida – Fiction   I. Title.
PS-------   T --------------   ------------------

Cover credit: Painting the "Air Nymph" by Kevin Clark   www.kc-art.com

Prologue

It's not often that a writer is fortunate enough to experience something in his life, that is so heart-wrenching that it burns deeply in his gut until the events are finally put down on paper.

At 4:17 A.M. on March 1, 2005 I was fortunate enough to be sitting at my mother's hospital bedside holding her hand as she took her final breath. I spent four nights sleeping in a very uncomfortable chair holding her hand as she battled with a virulent strain of pneumonia that filled up her lungs and sapped her will to live. In her last days she proved to me that she was much stronger than I.

The Friday afternoon before that fateful day she told me, the attending nurse in the Intensive Care Unit and her doctor that she wanted no more tubes in her lungs, no more IV's in her arms and no more medications. I cried when she made that decision, but she didn't. She winked at me, smiled and whispered softly, "I'm going to be with Dad. Are my affairs all in order?"

I croaked out a feeble 'yes' squeezed her hand and mumbled. "Mom, go and be with Dad. It's okay. You can go now."

However, she didn't make that trip on Friday and suffered through four long nights of pain and mental anguish. I'm certain that the morphine administered numbed the physical pain, but her mental senses remained sharp. She was always aware of her surroundings and those around her. On Saturday I gathered the immediate family members at her bedside for their final goodbye. She knew why they were there and her knowing made me cry.

It all started the prior Sunday when I brought her home from the hospital after a ten-day stay caused by bronchial pneumonia. The visiting nurse visited her Monday and I stopped by after work after purchasing her favorite literary publications - the *National Inquirer* and *The Globe* of course. When I called her at

9:00 P.M. Tuesday to ask how she was doing she responded, "Not very good." I should have known what was ahead. She did.

I called her the next morning at nine o'clock and she didn't answer the telephone. Hoping that she was in the bathroom I waited and re-dialed at 9:05. When the telephone was finally picked up it sounded like it hit the floor and she didn't answer with a cheery 'hello'. Instead I heard a 'gurgling' sound and a series of grunts.

I mumbled, "Hold on mom. I'll be right there." I flew out of my office like a rocket off its launching pad and made the seven-mile trip through heavy mid-morning traffic from Stuart to Port St. Lucie in twelve minutes.

I arrived at her house I unlocked the front door and ran to the master bedroom. My mother was thrashing around in her bed and her hands arms and legs trembled uncontrollably. I shouted "Hang on" and ran for the telephone to dial 911. The paramedics made it there in less than five minutes and she was in the Emergency Room five minutes after that.

When they allowed me to see her four hours later she was wired up to machines and several clear plastic tubes ran through her mouth into her lungs. Oxygen flowed in from one tube and frothy, blood-saturated fluid flowed out of the other tube. Blood and spittle ran down the left side of her ashen face.

"Mom, I'm here," I whispered. She opened her eyes and the look she gave me made me think of a cocker spaniel hit by a car and lying helpless in the road with a broken back. She couldn't speak, but later in Intensive Care she spelled out, "Did I die?" on an alphabetical fingerboard. I lied and told her 'no."

The total experience, although horrendous, and mind boggling was so captivating that I stopped work on *Treasure Coast JADE* and penned this story. Now I feel complete.

I wish to thank the doctors, nurses and staff members of the Port St. Lucie Medical Center all of whom shared my grief with me. I also wish to thank my wife Michi for her understanding throughout my tribulations and the tortuous creation of this work.

Paul McElroy

Dedication

I wish to dedicate this humble work to my mother Betty Jean McElroy who left this mortal earth at 4:17 A.M., March 1, 2005 while I sat at her hospital bedside and held her hand. She shared her most sacred secrets and fears with me in those final hours.

After knowing her for sixty-two years it was only at the time of her passing that I finally knew and understood my mother for who she was. However, I still wonder if she ever really knew and understood me for who I am. I hope so. This book is for you.

Thank you mom for the things that you did for me and for the twenty-nine days and nights you spent at my hospital bedside while I was in a coma, inflicted with Equine Encephalitis and considered to be brain dead. I sat by your side as you sat by mine.

If it was not for your guidance and wisdom I may have taken another path down the Road of Life and be someone other than the person I am. I sincerely hope that I am worthy of your legacy.

Your grateful and adoring son,

Also by Paul E. McElroy

Treasure Coast DECEIT
ISBN 0-9715136-0-0
January 2002

Treasure Coast Archipelago
ISBN 0-9715136-1-9
March 2003

Treasure Coast GOLD
ISBN 0-9715136-2-7
January 2004

Treasure Coast ENIGMA
ISBN 0-9715136-3-5
September 2004

Chapter

1

It was 1:17 A.M. on Monday when I stepped into the elevator on the second floor of the hospital. It had been a tough day and I was finishing up my night rounds. I was well behind my normal schedule because of a death in the Intensive Care Unit. I was anxious to finish up my rounds and get a hot cup of coffee when the hospital cafeteria opened at six o'clock. Several critical patients on the second floor held me up because they wanted to know what they could expect and in return what was expected of them. Those delicate consultations took an hour that I didn't have to spare.

The elevator car came to a jerky stop on the third floor directly in front of the oval-shaped nurses' station, the door slid open and I stepped out into the hallway. The nurses didn't pay any attention to the opening of the elevator door. They were busy making entries in patients' charts, making small talk and discussing patients' situations with concerned husbands, wives and other immediate family members. None of the nurses harbored any thoughts of becoming a local Florence Nightingale and were used to the routine of administering medications, taking vital sign readings, adjusting catheters, emptying waste bags and assuring dying patients and their anxious families that everything would be alright although they knew better.

"Has anyone checked on the pneumonia patient in Room 310?" Asked Jeanne, an RN, and very experienced supervising duty nurse.

"I stuck my head in her room about five minutes ago and she was snoring like an Iowa hog," responded Hazel an experienced LPN who wore her blonde hair in a ponytail. "She's out of it."

"When she wakes up the pain will still be there," Jeanne replied. 'She's trying to put on a tough face in front of us, but she should be spared pain. What dose did her doctor order?"

"Originally two milligrams every three hours, or as needed."

"What have you been giving her?"

"I'll check her chart," replied Debbie a rookie Phillipino nurse who had graduated from nursing school two weeks earlier and was anxious to please. "Here it is! Her last injection was at ten-thirty and it was four milligrams."

"She asked me to increase her dosage at eight-thirty because she couldn't stand the pain," Hazel responded as she ignored Debbie's comment. "I called her doctor and he ordered changing it from two milligrams to four milligrams."

"When she wakes up ask her if she has any pain and if she does give her what she needs," the duty nurse ordered. "Ask her some questions and determine if she's lucid. Morphine can cause weird effects in some patients."

"According to her chart she has double pneumonia and isn't expected to last the night," Debbie chipped in.

"But we have to keep her as comfortable and pain free as we can," Hazel responded with a frown to indicate her displeasure at the rookie for interfering in her patient's business.

"I agree," Jeanne replied. " Is anyone with her?"

"Her son. He sleeps in a chair beside her bed every night. He doesn't want her to die alone."

"That's nice."

I slowly sauntered over to the patient status board mounted on the wall behind the nurses' station and scanned the room numbers and patient names. A colored dot made with a dry erasable marker indicated the status of each patient. A doctor could quickly determine a patient's status by glancing at the status board. A green dot meant that the patient had the possibility of recovery. A yellow dot indicated that the patient was in a slowly declining condition and not expected to last more than three days. A blue dot indicated a critical condition requiring periodic injections of morphine to control the pain of the dying patient and a complete cut off of their normal medications. A red dot indicated that death was imminent and the patient was not to be resuscitated. The nurses also carried a code for each patient on the backside of their identification badge.

"Does anybody besides me feel a draft in here?" Asked Debbie the rookie Phillipino nurse. "I just felt a chill like someone opened a window."

"You'll get used to it," responded Jeanne the duty nurse. It happens every night about this time. The rooms get real cold no matter where we set the thermostat. I think that the maintenance people work on the central air conditioning system between two and four o'clock in the morning."

"Has anyone said anything to them about it?"

"It doesn't make any difference. A doctor told me that the cold temperature keeps down the bacteria count and it's better for the patients."

"Do you think Emma will show up tonight?" Hazel asked with a wide grin on her face.

"She was here earlier," responded Marilyn a brunette, petite LPN with a butch brush cut.

"Did you see her?" Hazel was planting a seed and wanted Debbie to take the bait. Marilyn decided to play along and upped the ante.

"I felt her presence when I checked the patient in Room 303 about one-thirty."

"Didn't that patient pass away?"

"Yes. She had terminal lung cancer and she passed about one forty-five."

"Did you open the window to let her spirit out?" Blurted out Hazel. "If you didn't it could mean trouble for us tonight!"

"I was with her when she passed and I opened the window for her," Marilyn responded. "She smiled when she took her last breath and turned toward the window like she wanted to escape. She did and it's okay. She won't bother us."

The experienced nurses seemed unconcerned and went back to recording data in their patient's charts. Debbie, shocked by what she had just heard, sat in her seat with her mouth open as if she wanted to say something, but didn't know what would make any sense to her peers.

I would like to stay and see how far the conversation would go, but I had rounds to make and I didn't need for the nurses to get in my way. I glanced at the patient status board, scanned each room number, read the patient's last name and mentally recorded their condition code. The most critical patients were assigned to Rooms 301 and 310 because they are the closest rooms to the nurses' station.

The name of the patient in Room 301 is Brown. The sex code indicated 'F' for female and status code is red and not a good sign for her. I elected not to engage the nurses in conversation, glanced through the blue notebook labeled '301' and read the diagnosis and prognosis of Linda Brown.

Linda is a white female, thirty-five years of age and suffers from terminal cervical cancer. She is being administered morphine to numb her pain and sugar water as needed to quench her thirst.

I decided to check on Linda first because she didn't have much time. The pony-tailed blonde nurse looked in my direction, but didn't acknowledge my presence. Without a doubt she had seen me making my night rounds before and knew that I prefer to be alone when I'm interviewing a patient. I shook the cobwebs out of my brain and shuffled towards Room 301.

Chapter
2

Room 301 was lit only by the small crack of light that oozed out of the gap under the bathroom door. It didn't matter to me. I didn't need very much light to read Linda's body language and find out if she was ready for the painful journey ahead. I read the nurses' notations in her file and knew that her blood pressure was averaging 120 over 90 and that her pulse rate was 72 beats per minute. Her white blood cell count was twenty-one thousand per micro liter. That extremely high count clearly indicated the ferocity with which the invading cancer cells were attacking and destroying her vital organs.

I paused at Linda's bedside and watched the corners of her mouth twitch as she reacted to the overpowering twinges of pain that came from deep within her body. The large doses of morphine dulled the pain and put her into an almost euphoric state of mind. I needed to speak with her and to do so I had to wake her up.

"Linda," I softly called out to her. "Linda, please wake up. I need to speak with you about your pain and what I can do for you."

Her eyes fluttered softly and slowly opened as a slight smile of recognition shone through the pain and sense-dulling morphine fog.

"Hello doctor. I remember you from last night. Why are you back tonight?"

"I wanted to spend some more time with you and discuss some treatment options."

"I know that I'm dying and the only treatment I need is something to stop the pain."

"The nurse will be in here in a few minutes to give you an injection. How do you feel?"

"Like crap! I'm ready for this to be over. How long is it going to take?"

"That depends upon you. If you feel that you're ready to go just close your eyes and slowly drift away. There's nothing to be afraid of. I'll stand here and hold your hand if that will help you."

"That would be nice. I'm ready to go."

"Linda, before you take that step will you spend a few minutes telling me about your self?"

"What do you want to know?"

"Who you are, where you came from, how you fit in with your family, what you did with your life and what you still want to accomplish."

"I don't think that I'm going to accomplish much more of anything except to die and get this thing over with. It isn't any fun."

"I know that it's difficult, but it's a journey you must make alone and the pain will be gone."

"How do you know that?"

"Know what Linda?"

"That the pain will be gone? I don't want to spend eternity in pain."

"When the physical body dies there can be no pain because there are no nerve endings left to transmit pain impulses to the brain."

"What about the brain? Does it feel pain?"

"No. The brain feels no pain because there are no pain receptors in the brain itself. It only translates and interprets pain impulses from parts of the body."

"Oh."

"Linda tell me a little something about yourself."

"What do you want to know?"

"Give me a short biographical overview."

"Are you writing my obituary?"

"No. That's someone else's job. I'm a doctor. Tell me where you were born, where you went to school, what jobs you held during your career and your unfulfilled dreams."

"Can I go after that? I'm ready. You make me feel very relaxed."

"Of course you can."

"Okay. I'm thirty-five years old and I was born in Hoffman Estates, Illinois, that's a suburb about twenty-five miles northwest of Chicago."

"I'm familiar with the area."

"I graduated from Hoffman Estates High School and went to the University of Illinois in Champaign."

"What was your major?"

"I earned a Master's Degree in Advertising."

"I suspect that you were an excellent student."

"I was. My Grade Point Average was three point eight."

"Did you find a good job after you graduated from college?"

"Yes! I was hired by an electronics manufacturing company based in Elgin to do their public relations work and develop their advertising campaign."

"How far did you go in your career?"

"I won three *ADDIES for* my advertising campaigns and was promoted to vice president of marketing last year. I got sick right after I was promoted. It's been downhill since then."

"Tell me about your family."

"My father's an engineer with Motorola in Schaumburg and my mother's just a housewife."

"That's a full time job in itself. Do you have any brothers or sisters?"

"No. I'm an only child."

"Are you married?"

"No. Never been and don't want to either."

"Do your parents know how ill you are?"

"No. I haven't told them. They'll find out when I'm gone."

"Don't you want them to be here with you? You could use some family support while you are going through this transition."

"They haven't considered me to be a member of their family for several years. We haven't spoken since they found out."

"Found out what? That you have cervical cancer?"

"No, since they found out that I'm a lesbian."

"What?"

"That's right. I'm a lesbian and darn proud of it. My father thinks that I'm a pervert and my mother won't even discuss it with me but that's okay. I reconciled myself to a life of loneliness and I have no regrets."

"What about your partner? Where is she?"

"I don't know where the bitch is. She split with a fat broad from Key West a month after I got sick."

"Oh. Do you have any unfulfilled dreams? Things that you wanted to do and were never able to?"

"Of course. Don't you?"

"I imagine that I do. But I've never thought about it."

"Then why did you ask me if I did?"

"It seemed to be the right thing to do and I wanted to know more about you before you pass."

"So! You are writing my obituary aren't you?"

"No, I'm not writing your obituary. I just wanted to get to know you a little better. Is there anything that you want to tell me before you pass?"

"So, now you are a priest and I suppose that you want me to confess my sins?"

"No, I'm not a priest, a rabbi, a minister or any of those things. I'm just a country doctor making his late night rounds and getting to know his patients. How's your pain now?"

"I don't have any and I feel pretty darn good. I might be able to walk out of here tonight. Did you slip a needle in my arm when I wasn't looking?"

"No. I didn't, but what you're feeling is a normal reaction. It's an endorphin rush."

"What's that?"

"It's a rush of chemical signals that the brain sends out to the body telling it that everything is going to be fine."

"Does that mean that I'm getting better?"

"Do you want me to be honest with you?"

"Of course. I'm a big girl and I can handle it."

"Your brain is in a panic because it senses that your body is in the final stages of death and it is telling the body to hang on. But it can't."

"Oh. Just because I feel better doesn't mean that I'm getting better?"

"No, it's just the opposite. Your body is using up the last bit of energy that it has left. It won't be long now."

"Will it hurt when I die?"

"No, it will be very peaceful. When you're ready tell your spirit that you're ready to go and it will softly whisk you away to a much better place. Before you go tell the nurse to open the window."

"Why?"

"Some of the nurses believe that a person's soul cannot escape their body unless the window is left open at the time of death. You don't want your spirit to be trapped in this room for eternity do you?"

"No! Can you open the window for me now?"

"Are you ready to go?"

"I think so. Are you going to stay with me?"

"If you want me to I'll stay. Do you want me to hold your hand?"

"Yes! "

"Okay. How does that feel?"

"Are you holding my hand?"

"Yes I am."

"I can't feel it."

"Linda, it's time for you to go."

"I know. Did you open the window?"

"Yes I did."

"Will you be there when I get there?"

"Not tonight. Maybe later. I still have a lot of patients to see tonight."

"Goodbye Linda."

"Goodbye doctor."

Chapter
3

Two anxious nurses, Marilyn and Debbie, were poised outside of Linda's room as I exited. A light breeze drifted through the room and wafted into the hallway. They ignored me and went about their business of preparing medications that Linda no longer needed.

"Did you feel that breeze?" Nurse Debbie remarked as she adjusted the screen of the laptop computer mounted on top of the medication dispenser cart.

"Yes. I did," Marilyn replied. "Maybe someone opened the window for her?"

"Who could have done that? She hasn't had any visitors."

"A doctor came through here a little while ago. Maybe he opened it for her."

"I don't think so. They aren't that smart. Marilyn, did you bring the patient's chart?"

"No. It wasn't on the shelf. Why?"

"I wanted to check her morphine dosage level. She hasn't been doing very well for the last few hours and it might be time to increase her dosage. It wouldn't be fair for her to suffer pain at the end."

"A doctor must have picked up her chart when we weren't looking. They never put things back where they're supposed to go. Men! We're always picking up their mess! Do you want me to go back for it?"

"Naw. It's not important. Let's check her vitals first. If she's comfortable we'll give her the same level we did last time. If she's hurting I don't have any problem goosing her levels up a little bit if it will make her more comfortable."

"Deb, I'm ready to go. Are you?"

"No problem. Let's get this over with."

The nurses pushed the drug cart into Linda's room and didn't look up to acknowledge that I was there. This was going to be a long night for everyone, but fortunately for Linda it was over.

After the two somber nurses entered the room, I heard Debbie remark, "Marilyn, it looks like she's gone. Does she have a DNR on file?"

"Yes. I checked her file for it when we came on shift at seven o'clock."

"Marilyn! Don't forget to open the window!"

"It's already open Deb. Did you open it?"

"No."

"That's where the breeze came from when we were yakking in the hall. You'd better get Jeanne down here to double-check her vitals. I'll start taking the IV's out of her arms."

"Okay."

I stood in the corridor outside of Linda's room and watched the other nurses bustling in and out of their patient's rooms. I needed a few minutes to gain my composure before I entered the next room. It isn't easy to watch someone die no matter how many times you've seen it happen. I hoped that Linda's spirit found its way out of the open window into the cool night air.

I mentally ran through the diagnosis and prognosis of the patient in Room 302. I didn't need to return to the nurses' station to pull the chart. I remembered the most important data.

Ralph Thomas was fifty-seven years old and in the final stages of prostate cancer. At 6' 4" and 245 pounds since his senior year in high school Ralph had been a robust athlete and played in a community softball league until just a few months ago when his strength was sapped by the cancer. Now he only weighed 155 pounds and couldn't walk more than a few steps without help.

He attended MIT on an academic scholarship, earned a Masters Degree in computer science and graduated at the top of his class. He went to work at IBM as a computer engineer right out of college and helped to develop bubble memory matrixes. He worked at IBM for 30 years and retired two years ago at age 55. He bought a nice house on the water in Palm City and bought a fifty-eight foot Hatteras sportfishing yacht for trips to the Bahamas.

Ralph never married, his parents were killed in an automobile accident seven years ago and he has no brothers or sisters. He never made out a Will and he's concerned about who will get his money and property when he's gone.

Ralph's aggressive cancer moved to his brain and he is often incoherent. I hope that he's in a mood to communicate with me because his dreams may be cut short this night.

I took a deep breath, rubbed the right side of my nose with my right index finger for luck and headed for the door of Room 302.

Chapter

4

I tried to slip silently through the open door, but I must have made a noise because Ralph stirred and his ruddy face broke into a broad smile when he saw me. His thinning red hair had no mass or shape and stood straight up from his skull as if it was heavily jelled. That didn't seem to matter to him.

When Ralph saw me he sat up in bed as best he could and greeted me. "Hello Doc! It's about time you got here. I expected to see you about two hours ago."

"I got hung up on the second floor with a couple of new patients. How're you doing tonight?"

"Not too good Doc. Pull up a chair and tell me what's going on with you."

"I think I will," I answered as I pulled a standard hospital chair next to his bed. "So, tell me about your softball league. What place are you guys in this year?"

"We were in first place when I dropped out. I just couldn't keep up with the young kids anymore."

"I know what you mean. I find it difficult to make my rounds every night."

"It's better than the alternative."

"I suppose so. Ralph, did you see Emma come through tonight?"

"Doc, you know that she always comes through here at the same time every night. When that elevator opens at exactly one-seventeen and nobody's on it those nurses know that Emma's back. She's hasn't missed a night since I've been in here."

"Did she say anything to you?"

"Nope. She slipped right past me, went over to the window and opened it just a crack. She held her finger up to her lips and winked at me as she glided out of the room. Can you feel the breeze?"

"Yes. Ralph, are you cold? I can close the window for you."

"No! Leave it open. I almost feel like I could slip out of this old body and fly away on the wind. I'm tired of the pain. This isn't any fun."

"I understand."

"Doc, how could you possibly understand what I'm going through?"

"I've been making night rounds in this hospital for twenty-two years and I've seen everything. You might be surprised if you knew what I've seen in all those years."

"How long has Emma been coming through here?"

"About three years. Why do you ask?"

"Is she a ghost?"

"No. She's a spirit."

"A spirit! Isn't that the same as a ghost?"

"Not really. A ghost is the spirit of a person who is unable to rest and can't leave the location. Sometimes they act as guards or sentinels. Emma is a trapped spirit that can't leave. She's trying to find her way out of the hospital, but she never will. She'll be here for Eternity."

"What do you mean trapped?"

"Emma died on this floor and there was a new nurse on duty

who didn't know that she was supposed to open the window to allow Emma's spirit to escape. So, her spirit's trapped here."

"Why doesn't she just go out the front door?"

"She can't. Her spirit thinks that it's her job is to roam the hospital halls and open the window for every dying patient so their spirit doesn't get trapped in the hospital like hers did."

"That sounds pretty far-fetched. How do you know?"

'She told me."

"Emma talked to you? She never says anything to me when she passes through my room."

"She talks to me all the time and she doesn't need to say anything to the patients. You should feel comfortable that she is here looking out for you."

"Doc, she opened my window. Does that mean what I think it does?"

"Yes. She's helping you. Are you ready to go?"

"Yes! I'd do anything to get rid of this pain and this screwed up body of mine isn't worth two cents. Can you help me?"

"No, that would be against the law. But, you can help yourself."

"How?"

"Close your eyes, relax and will yourself to go. If your mind's ready your body will follow."

"I can't relax. My mind's all keyed up."

"Why? Is there something bothering you? Your mind has to be clear before you can go."

"What's going to happen to my house, my boat and my money?"

"You aren't planning on taking it with you are you? That might be just a little difficult to accomplish."

"No. I know that I can't take it with me, but I don't have any family to leave it to! Who gets it?"

"Do you have a Will?"

"Yes. I made one out when I found out that I had the big 'C'."

"Where is it?"

"In my safe deposit box."

"Who knows that it's in there?"

"My attorney."

"Does he know that you're in the hospital?"

"Yes."

"Then he'll take care of your Will for you and your last wishes. Whom did you leave your things to?"

"I want my house and boat to be sold and the proceeds to go to Big Brothers and Sisters, plus all of my cash."

"If that's what's in your Will your attorney will make certain that your wishes are followed to the letter."

"Will you check on it for me?"

"Of course, but if you stay on good behavior you might be able to finagle old St. Peter into a trip back here to check on everything. Then you can rest in peace."

"I'm going to be cremated. Does it hurt?"

"Of course it doesn't hurt," I couldn't hold back a slight chuckle as I answered. "Your spirit is already out of your body. Don't worry. You won't feel a thing."

"Will it hurt when I die?"

"No. You'll just fall asleep. It will be very peaceful."

"I guess I'm ready then. I feel a lot better. Will you stay here with me?"

"Of course. Do you want me to open the window a little bit more? You're a big man." I rose and headed for the window.

"That's a good idea. I don't feel very big anymore, but I don't want to scrape my buns on the way out. I bruise easily."

"Okay. It's not very cold outside tonight. I'll open it up all the way. That will make it easy for you. I wouldn't want you to leave a hanging part of your anatomy on the edge of the window. That metal's sharp."

"Thanks. Doc, if its okay with you I think I'll doze off now. I'm pooped."

"You go right ahead. I'll stand right here until you doze off."

"Doc! Look outside in the hall! Emma's outside my room!"

I turned around quickly, faced the open door and could see into the hall. I didn't see anything unusual.

"Do you see her Doc?"

"Of course I do."

"She's just standing there looking at me and smiling."

"Is she saying anything to you?"

"No. She's got her arms crossed and she's smiling at me."

"What do you think it means?"

"I think she's waiting for me to come over."

"I agree. She knows that I opened the window for you. Her job's done."

"Doc, I wish I could stay here and talk to you all night, but I know that it's time for me to go. Do you mind?"

"Of course not Ralph. Is there anything that you want me to do for you while you are making the transition?"

"This might sound silly, but would you hold my hand? I'm not a sissy but I might want you to pull me back if I don't like it on the other side when I get there."

"No problem. How will I know if you want me to pull you back? You have to give me a signal."

"I'll jerk on your hand three times."

"Okay, give me your hand." I took Ralph's right hand in my own and placed my left hand on top of his hand. His skin was cool to the touch. "Okay Ralph, you can go now."

There was no response. I looked at Ralph's face. His eyes were closed and he was smiling. A slight breeze rushed past my face on its way through the open window.

"Goodbye Ralph. Have a good trip."

I placed Ralph's hand gently onto his chest, patted it softly three times, turned to leave and stopped in my tracks. Emma stood in the open doorway, smiled and faded into nothingness. Ralph was gone and Emma was pleased. Her job was done.

Chapter
5

I'm a professional and I know better than to show emotions in front of a patient. I slipped out of Ralph's room as silently as I had entered. Two nurses were hustling down the hall towards Ralph's room. Apparently the pulse monitor alarm had sounded and they were on the way with the intent of preventing Ralph from making his escape.

I caught a 'flit' of movement out of the corner of my right eye and I turned my head to the right. Emma was doing a graceful pirouette in the hallway in front of Room 303. She winked, blew me a soft kiss off the open palm of her left hand and danced through the doorway. A slight breeze wafted down the hall and settled on my right cheek. I knew that I had to follow her, but I had forgotten the patient's name and condition. I needed to make a trip to the nurses' station and review the patient status board.

"Cathy, do you think that Mr. Thomas is playing games

again?" Asked Mary Beth a stocky, redheaded nurse that could pass for a middle linebacker on a woman's football team. "Last night he pulled off his monitoring cuff and stuck it under his pillow. When I flew into his room with the crash cart he was laying there with his mouth and eyes wide open staring at the ceiling. When I reached down to close his eyes and he sat up and hollered 'boo!' I almost crapped my pants!"

"He thinks that he's a joker, but he doesn't realize that we have a lot of very sick patients up here," responded Cathy an obviously disgusted middle-aged blonde LPN. "I warned him that I'd give him an enema that he won't forget for a long time if he keeps it up."

"Make it a warm prune juice enema!"

"Why prune juice?"

"It acts fast and it's very messy. He won't ever forget it. Cathy, are you ready to go?"

"Yep. Does he have a DNR order on file?"

"I don't think so. If he did there would be a DNR sticker on his door."

"Mary Beth, should I check his chart?"

"Naw. If he's gone then he's gone. We need the bed for a gal down in ICU anyway. Let's leave the cart out here and check his vitals first."

"Okay."

The two nurses cautiously entered the dimly lit room fully expecting the patient to sit up in bed and holler 'boo' at them. "Mr. Thomas. Are you still with us?" Mary Beth inquired in a soft whisper.

I drifted to the left and down the hallway towards the centrally located nurses' station. Emma was nowhere in sight. Three nurses were conferring over a multi-colored computer screen when I walked up and Jeanne the supervising RN was pointing at a red bar graph.

"Marilyn, it shows right here that you gave the patient four milligrams of morphine less than an hour ago. Are you certain that you gave him the entire injection?"

"Of course I did!"

"We had a problem with you over the administering of patient meds the last time you filled in for someone else! Did you hold some of the morphine back for yourself?"

"Jeanne, are you accusing me of being a druggie?"

"Didn't you go through three weeks of rehab?"

"Yes, but that was because of stress. I couldn't fall asleep after a shift and it helped me to relax. I don't need drugs!"

"No one here needs or gets drugs except the patients under our care. If you are certain that you gave him the full four milligrams then his pain must be very severe. I'll call his doctor and ask him if he'll authorize either increasing the dosage or allowing us to shoot him up at shorter intervals."

"Why don't you call his doctor and ask him to authorize a morphine drip? That way you can be certain that I'm clean?"

"I will. Would you please go down and check on the patient in Room 303? I heard her coughing her head off a few minutes ago and her lungs might be hemorrhaging. Her name's Beth."

"What's her problem?"

"Chronic emphysema and congestive heart failure. Her lungs are filling up fast. She declined a respirator and lung suction to clean them out. She might have to go on morphine before our shift is over. She's trying hard to hold on until her mother gets here from Louisville, Kentucky."

"When is she coming in?"

"Beth told me that she'd be here tomorrow afternoon. But, I don't think that Beth can hang on that long and she doesn't want to be awake when her lungs fill up. She knows that she is going to drown in her own body fluid."

"What do you want me to tell her?"

"Check her vitals and do a blood/oxygen test. If her oxygen level is below ninety-two percent increase the oxygen in her direct flow and if she's awake offer her morphine. Her doctor authorized four milligrams every three hours. Tell her that it will make her relax and allow her to breathe easier."

"But it will slow down her respiration rate! Her lungs will fill up faster."

"I know. But that's the way it goes in the big city."

'That's a mean attitude!"

"So, Florence Nightingale, what suggestions do you have? Do

we allow her to cough the lining out of her lungs? That wouldn't be pretty would it?"

"No. I'll do it," the miffed nurse responded as she spun on her heel and headed in the direction of Room 303. She knew that she would be able to siphon off two milligrams of morphine for herself.

"*I need to calm down*," Marilyn thought. "*That last hit didn't do a thing for me.*"

I turned toward the patient status board and made some mental notes. The patient was a white female and her name was Beth Adams. There was a red dot beside her name. I pulled out her chart and scanned the cover page. Beth was fifty-three years old, a chronic smoker and suffered from emphysema since childhood.

"*She should have known better than to smoke*," I thought. "*She issued her own death sentence.*"

Beth's chart indicated that she was admitted to the Emergency Room three days earlier suffering from lack of breath and chest pains. She woke up at home, saw that her fingernails were blue and called 911. The Emergency Room staff determined that she suffered from oxygen deprivation and was in the early stages of bronchial pneumonia. She was moved to the Intensive Care Unit the same day and transferred to the third floor yesterday afternoon.

There was little hope for Beth as the short-term prognosis was for the pneumonia to worsen. I replaced Beth's chart in the proper slot, took a deep breath and headed for Room 303.

The nurses ignored me and went about their normal duties interspersed with calls from children, husbands and suitors. It was going to be a long night for everyone on the third floor.

Chapter
6

By the time I made it to the open doorway of Room 303 Emma had already departed and was dancing all by herself in the hallway. She didn't need a partner. She swirled, dipped and pirouetted to an unseen audience. She smiled at me, curtsied twice and danced away in the direction of Room 304.

The television set blared out of the open doorway and was loud enough to keep everyone on the floor awake if they weren't in a morphine-induced fog. Beth seemed to be sleeping. Her long auburn hair was spread across the white pillow under her head and formed a glimmering halo. I stood in the doorway and gazed at her.

"*Why do bad things always seem to happen to good people?*" I asked myself. "*She doesn't deserve to die like this.*"

Beth seemed to hear my thoughts, stirred and her eyes opened.

"*Her green eyes look like glowing emeralds,*" I thought.

"They're beautiful."

"Hello doctor," she whispered softly as if she was afraid of waking up other patients. "Isn't it kind of late for you to be making hospital rounds?"

"I got hung up in ICU. A couple of new patients wanted to talk to me. Did I wake you?"

"No. I was just dozing. The television set makes me sleepy."

"Do you mind if I turn it off? It might be a little loud for everyone else."

"Of course. I'm a little hard of hearing and I might have the volume turned up a little to high."

"Beth, would you like to talk to me?"

"Yes. I don't think that I have much time left. I'm hanging on because my mother will be here tomorrow." She coughed from deep within her tiny chest, rolled over and spit out a yellow glob of mucous from her lungs into a tissue. "It's getting worse. The mucous is getting thicker and thicker."

"That's to be expected."

"But I'm going to get better and I'm going to walk out of this place under my own power. You'll see. I'm going to quit smoking and I'm moving to Tempe, Arizona where there's no humidity. I'm going to start an exercise program and get my lungs back in shape. My lungs will clear up. You'll see."

"I bet they will in short order."

"Beth, would tell me a little about yourself?"

"Why?"

"I like to learn as much about my patients as I can. It helps me to understand them better."

"What would you like to know?"

"Where were you born? Where did you go to school? What did your parents do for a living? What were your dreams? What did you accomplish and where do you think you failed?"

"I was born in Louisville, Kentucky. I went to the University of Kentucky and dropped out after two years. My father was a coal miner and my mother stayed home and drank."

"Why did you drop out of college? Did you have financial problems?"

"No. I was there on an academic scholarship. I got drunk at a frat party and wound up pregnant."

"What about the baby's father?"

"What about him?"

"Didn't he offer to marry you or help you out?"

"I didn't know who he was. It was a pretty wild party and I went to a lot of frat parties."

"What did your parents say about you getting pregnant?"

"Nothing. I didn't tell them. I never went home after that. I couldn't face them."

"What about the baby?"

"I never had it. I got an abortion. The frat boys chipped in for me."

"Did you go back to college?"

"No. Back in those days nobody wanted used merchandise. The frat boys loved to party with me, but they wouldn't take me home to meet their momma."

"What did you do?"

"I tried being a waitress in an off-campus bar, but the frat guys kept hitting on me. I got tired of the pickup scene, quit and moved to Miami."

"What did you do there?

"I worked as a topless dancer in a bar on South Beach until my boobs went flat. They don't like saggy boobs down there. The place is full of beautiful people and if you're not perfect you don't fit."

"Did you ever get married?"

"How do you expect a topless dancer with flat, saggy boobs to ever get married?"

"I apologize."

"No. I never got married."

"How did you make ends meet?"

"I suppose that you think that I turned into a hooker don't you?"

"I never said that."

"But you were thinking it weren't you?"

"No. What did you do after you left Miami Beach?"

"I didn't leave there right away. I took a job in the marina behind the Biscayne Bay Marriott."

"Did you drive boats?"

"No. You need a Coast Guard license to drive boats. I was a deckhand."

"What's that?"

"I tended to the passengers' needs during the cruise and cleaned the boat up after each trip."

"Oh."

"What do you mean by that?"

"By what?"

"The deep sigh and the oh. Do you think that I was servicing the male passengers?'

"Of course not. I figured that you served in the same capacity as a flight attendant on an airplane."

"That's close."

"Tell me about your father."

"Why?"

"I'd like to know about him."

"He died in a coal mine accident ten years ago and my mother re-married a used car salesman."

"Were you close to your father?"

"Hell no! The bastard started slipping into my bedroom and molesting me when I was only ten years old."

"What about your mother?"

"What about her?"

"Did you tell her what your father was doing to you? She could have stopped him."

"No. I didn't tell her. It would've broke her heart and it wouldn't have done any good."

"Why not?"

"She was drunk by nine o'clock every night and usually passed out on the couch. She didn't care."

"I understand from the nurse that your mother is on the way to see you. She'll be here tomorrow."

"Maybe she'll make it in time and maybe she won't. She had a stroke a few years ago, is in a wheelchair and it's hard for her to travel. I don't care one way or the other."

"Do you have any brothers or sisters?"

"Nope. It's just me. After I was born my mother had a

hysterectomy. That was a fortunate thing."

"Why do you say that?"

"Because God couldn't help me."

"Beth, it sounds as if you and your father had your differences, but is that a good reason for not getting along with your mother? After all she carried you for nine months and gave you life."

"I didn't ask to be born and I'm sorry that I was. This is no way to live."

"It's far too late to feel sorry for yourself. You made your own bed and now you must lie in it."

"I wasn't given the opportunity to live up to my potential and make something of myself. I could have really been somebody today if I'd finished college."

"It was your choice to attend wild frat parties. No one forced you to go and no one forced you to drink to excess."

"I didn't have a good role model! My mother was a drunk and my father molested me!"

"Those are excuses for your behavior and not reasons for your failure. You had choices and you made poor ones. No one is responsible for you getting drunk and having sex except yourself. If you wish I'll bring over a mirror so you can see the person responsible for your lot in life."

"You don't have to do that. I understand. How much longer do I have to suffer through this Hell? Can't you get one of those bimbos out there to give me something to make me just go to sleep? They wouldn't make a sick dog suffer like this."

"The best I can do is to ask them to increase your morphine dosage from two to four milligrams every three hours."

"Why not? You're a doctor aren't you?"

"I'm not your primary care physician. He makes all of your medication decisions. I'm just making night rounds so that the doctors who come in tomorrow morning will see my notes in their patient's charts."

"I know that one of those nurses isn't giving me the entire syringe full of morphine. She's holding back on me."

"Which one?"

"The lesbian broad with the brush cut and too much eye liner. Her name's Marilyn."

"What makes you think that she's shorting you? All of your medications are monitored via a computer that scans that bracelet on your wrist."

"The computer only knows that I was prescribed the morphine. It doesn't know how much was actually injected into my arm."

"What specifically makes you think that she is shorting you on your medication?"

"She's high most of the time. I heard her mumbling the last time she administered my morphine."

"What did you hear her say?"

"She thought I was sleeping and she said, 'Two for you and two for me makes Marilyn a happy girl.' That's why. The morphine wears off in about an hour and a half. Four milligrams is supposed to keep the pain away for three hours. Half the dose equals half the time. It's not hard math."

"I'll watch her the next time she gives you morphine. What time is your next injection?"

"She was here at three o'clock so I'm due again at six o'clock, if I last that long."

"You'll be here. Hold up your wrist so I can take your pulse."

"Why? I'm dying. If I have a pulse I'm still alive."

"Don't argue with me! Hold up your wrist," I repeated and reached for her arm. Her wrist was cold and clammy to the touch and her pulse rate was sixty-two beats per minute. It was a little slow indicating that her body was beginning to shut down. I placed the horn of my stethoscope to the left side of her emaciated chest. "Take a deep breath and exhale slowly," I directed and she complied.

There was a deep, bubbly rumble from her lungs when she exhaled indicating the buildup of fluid in her lungs. *"It won't be long now,"* I thought to myself. *"She's going to drown in her own body fluid and she knows it. Those nurses are going to have to keep her doped up to reduce the trauma."*

"Your lungs sound fine to me Beth," I glibly offered through my clenched teeth. I couldn't look her in the eye and she knew that I was lying.

"You lying bastard!" She screamed. "You know damn well

that my lungs are filling up and I'm going to drown like a rat in a toilet! You get your ass out there and tell that druggie nurse to shoot me out! I want to be out of it when I drown. I don't like pain and the thought of drowning turns me off in a big way!" She reached for my face with her outstretched claws.

I jumped back out of her way and headed for the door. "Okay! If that's the way you want it. I was just trying to help you, but with that kind of attitude I can't. You'll have to help yourself."

"I'm sorry," she replied. "Please come back and talk to me some more. I'm afraid of dying alone."

I stopped at the foot of her bed and looked her in the eye as I responded. "Beth, everyone is afraid of dying and we can't dictate when and where it's going to happen. You can't buy a ticket on the Death Train and it doesn't run on any schedule. When it happens it happens."

"But you're a doctor! Can't you give me something to make it easier?"

"No! That's against the law."

"What can you do then?" She leaned up on her left elbow and looked at me with the eyes of a dog hit by a car and lying in the road with a broken back. She knew that her time was near and she didn't want to face it by herself. I couldn't blame her. Facing Death is a frightening proposition for anyone.

"The best I can do is to ask Emma to see you. Do you feel that you're ready to make the journey?"

"Yes! Who's Emma? Is she another druggie nurse?"

"Emma's not a nurse. She's a facilitator."

"What's that?"

"Her role is to counsel and assist people like yourself to make the transition from life to death. I thought I saw her come out of your room a few minutes before I came in to see you."

"Do you mean that nice lady who opened the window for me?'

"That's her! Did she talk to you about anything?"

"She told me that everything was going to be fine and that when I was ready to go that I should look for her outside that window. I didn't understand that part. This room is on the third floor and there isn't a ledge or walkway out there. How can she stand outside the window?"

"Don't worry. Emma can do it."

"Is she a ghost or something?"

"She's a spirit that assists other spirits to find their way out of their human body when it's time for them to go. When you feel that you're ready to go look for Emma and let her guide you out of this room into a better place. Trust her. She'll know when you're ready before you do."

"I will. Thank you doctor." Beth closed her eyes, smiled and allowed her head to slowly fall back against the pillow.

I heard a soft tapping at the window and turned to see what it was. Emma was floating outside the window and she flashed me a Victory sign. I gave her thumbs up, turned and headed for the open door and the hallway. It was three twenty-four and I'd only seen three patients so far. I was running late.

I paused in the hall and overheard nurses Debbie and Jeanne discussing Beth's case.

"Deb, the radiologist who read her chest x-ray stopped by about eight o'clock to make some notes in her chart," Jeanne somberly said. "He told me that double pneumonia had set in and it was a matter of hours before her lungs started to fill up. Her primary care physician doesn't want her to die tonight and ordered a light morphine drip to keep her under. He wants us to keep her alive until her mother gets here tomorrow."

"Jeanne, it's already too late. She's gone."

Chapter
7

After spending time with Beth I didn't want to go into Room 304. The tiny patient, Kara Kuchenbecken, is nine years old and in the third grade. Her long blonde hair splayed out across the stark white pillow under her head and contrasted with the freckles on her nose. Her innocent face glowed radiantly like an angel's halo. She appeared to be at peace, but she was comatose. The virulent strain of brain cancer had done its irreparable damage to her delicate central nervous system.

When I entered her room Kara's sparkling cobalt blue eyes flickered, opened wide and she spoke in a clear unwavering voice. "I'm very happy doctor. I'm going to see everyone in my family very soon."

"What makes you think that?"

"My grandpa and grandma were sitting on the edge of my bed when you came into my room. They told me that they were here to guide my soul to Heaven. They left when you came in because they knew that you wanted to talk to me. Do you have something you wish to tell me?"

"No. I just stopped in as part of my normal rounds to check on how you're doing. Do you mind if I sit down on the edge of your bed?"

"Go right ahead," she responded as she gestured toward the bed with her hand. "I'm doing just fine. Ms. Emma was in to see me too. She's a nice lady."

"She certainly is. When was she here?"

"She left just before you came in. She told me that it was almost time for me to go. She opened the window so that my soul can escape when it's time for it to leave my sick body."

"What do you know about your condition? What have the doctors and nurses told you?"

"Nothing. They whisper to each other when they're in my room, but I can hear them talking out in the hall. I have a very aggressive form of brain cancer and it's untreatable. One of the cancer doctors suggested to my parents that they put me on chemotherapy and radiation treatment, but they said no. They knew that there is no hope and they wanted me to pass without pain and suffering. I feel no pain. Did you know that the brain has no nerve endings and can't feel pain?"

"I heard something about that in medical school. You used the word 'knew' when you spoke of your parents. Why didn't you use the word know? That's present tense."

"Because my parents were killed in an accident on I-ninety-five at four thirty-seven yesterday afternoon when they were on the way down from Fort Pierce to see me."

"Did one of the nurses tell you that?"

"How could they tell me anything? They think that I'm in a coma."

"Then how did you find out about it?"

"Mommy and daddy came to see me right after the accident. They sat right there on the edge of my bed where you're sitting and my daddy told me what happened. A big truck tried to pass my daddy's car and cut him off. Daddy lost control and the car went into a canal. Mommy and daddy both drowned. But it's okay. Daddy said that mommy was knocked unconscious when her head hit the windshield and she didn't feel anything. Daddy had the wind knocked out of him when his chest hit the steering wheel. When he tried to take a deep breath his lungs filled up with water, he lost consciousness and he drowned."

"I didn't see anything in your chart about your parents' deaths. I'm really sorry."

"It's okay. Mommy and daddy are with my grandma and grandpa right now. We'll all be together very soon. They're all waiting for me. Do you mind if I go now?"

"No. Go right ahead. If you're ready close your eyes and drift off. Ms. Emma will make certain that your spirit escapes the hospital."

"I know. She's floating outside the window right now. Doctor I have to go now. My grandma and grandpa came back and they're crying. They want me to go now."

"I see them. Have a good trip Kara."

"Thank you doctor. I will."

I took a deep breath, stood up and headed for the open door. Emma tapped on the window three times to get my attention. When I turned around Emma gave me a big smile and a 'thumbs up.' I gave her a 'thumbs up' back, turned and headed for the door. I knew nothing about this brave little girl and her hopes and dreams, but she was determined to be with her family.

"*So be it Emma!*" I mumbled. "*Take her now if you must, but be gentle to her tiny body and be extra kind to her soul. She has a long journey ahead of her.*"

Chapter

8

Two anxious nurses, Hazel and Mary Beth, hustled down the hallway toward little Kara's room. They were too late to help her and they knew it.

"Hazel, didn't you tell me that little girl was comatose?" Mary Beth, the short, squat, overweight middle-aged nurse, puffed out of pursed lips. "I distinctly heard talking coming out of that room when I walked past and it was a girl's voice!"

"She's been in a deep coma since yesterday afternoon," responded Hazel as the young, blonde pony-tailed nurse attempted to keep pace with Mary Beth's long strides, but no matter how hard she tried to match her companion's brisk pace their feet remained clumsily out of step. "Her doctor wanted to keep her doped up on a morphine drip until she passed."

"Why? She might have been able to ask for something."

"Her parents were killed in a car accident on I-95 yesterday afternoon about two miles north of the St. Lucie Boulevard exit ramp. They lived in Fort Pierce and were on the way here to see Kara when an eighteen-wheeler ran them off the road into a canal and they both drowned. The doctor felt it was better if she didn't know."

"Oh my God! How terrible! If she's gone at least she'll be with them now."

I stood outside Kara's room and slightly down the hall making notes on my clipboard as the two panic-stricken nurses entered her room. They were so concerned about Kara's condition and their responsibility that they paid no attention to me. A soft breeze gently brushed the left side of my face and was gone.

"*Thank you Kara,*" I softly mumbled as giant tears ran down both sides of my face. "*You're on your way now. Have a safe journey with your grandma and grandpa.*"

Chapter 9

After my short emotional visit with Kara I paused in the hallway and attempted to recover some of my professional composure. Courage often comes in small packages and that little girl has the courage of a mongoose! Emma was nowhere in sight and the nurses paid no attention to me. There was a flurry of activity in Kara's room as Jeanne, the nursing staff shift supervisor, came in to sign off on the time of death and gather information for her report.

After a few minutes I got my act together, managed to wipe off the traces of tears on my cheeks, sniffed a couple of times and headed for Room 305. I had no idea of what new challenges were ahead, but I'd reached my emotional saturation point for tonight.

"*Please dear God,*" I began to pray out loud and I'm not a religious person, "*Give me enough strength to continue. I still have to see six more patients on this floor and my nerves are shot.*" I peeked out of my left eye to see if Emma, or one of the nurses, was listening to my feeble pleas. No one was there and I doubted that God would show me any mercy. I broke a cardinal rule and became emotionally involved with a patient and lost my objectivity. I had to continue my rounds regardless of how I felt. Seriously ill patients were counting on me and Emma's work surely wasn't done.

It only took me seven steps to reach Door 305. Nurse Cathy and a white-haired elderly woman literally bolted out of the room and almost bowled me over in their haste. Neither of them bothered to excuse themselves and acted as if I wasn't even there.

"He told them not to come down here!" The elderly woman screamed at the nurse. "He doesn't want them to see him this way!"

"Mrs. Klinger, listen to me carefully! If your sons want to see their father before he passes away they'd better get down here quick. He doesn't have much time left."

"He told them to come down after it's over and take me back with them. Don't you understand! I've been sleeping on a cot in his room for the last five nights. I know what he wants!"

"I've watched you try to talk to him and he never responds. And you know that he can't. The doctors say that a portion of his brain suffered a lack of blood when he had the Grand Mal seizure and he is in a Persistent Vegetative State."

"I know that Elton can hear me! He responds to my voice!"

"Mrs. Klinger, listen to me! His last EKG was flat! He can't make health care decisions for himself, you are in no mental condition to do it for him and he doesn't have a Living Will. We have a legal obligation to keep him alive."

"His eyes are open and they follow me when I walk around the room."

"That's a normal reaction and does not mean that the cognitive part of his brain is functioning."

"What good will it do for me to call our sons?"

"They can tell us what they think their father wants and can give permission for us to insert a feeding tube in his stomach via his navel."

"No! He wouldn't want to live that way. He told me that

many times."

"Mrs. Klinger you haven't shown me a Living Will for your husband and my hands are tied." Nurse Cathy tugged on the elderly woman's left arm. "Let's go call your sons and tell them what's going on."

Mrs. Klinger grudgingly followed her in the direction of the nurses' station.

Fortunately for me a summary sheet from the patient's chart was attached to a clipboard stuffed in a plastic holder mounted on the wall beside the door. I reached for it and scanned the basic data entries.

The patient's name is Elton Klinger. He is a 65-year old white male suffering from an aggressive, inoperable brain tumor. His occupation is shown as nuclear engineer. He retired two months ago and moved to Port St. Lucie from Gretna, New Jersey. His wife of forty-five years Effie is at his bedside. He has two children, both sons, who live in New Jersey. He was admitted to the hospital yesterday afternoon after he had a grand mal seizure, lost control of his limbs and his wife called 911. He lost control of his body functions, including his bowels and bladder, two hours ago and he can't speak.

I hitched up my pants, cleared my throat and entered the room. Mr. Klinger's eyes were closed and he appeared to be asleep. I decided to test his senses with a simple question. "How are you feeling Elton?"

His eyes drifted slightly open and he squinted to see me better. He was obviously near-sighted and his gold-framed, wire-rimed glasses were on the bedside table.

He cautiously answered without opening his eyes completely. "Who are you?"

"I'm a doctor. I'm making late rounds and stopped in to check on you."

"Where's my wife?"

"She's out at the nurses' station conferring with the shift supervisor about your treatment."

"Can she hear us?"

"No."

"I'm not doing very good doc."

"That's what I see on your chart."

"I'm worried about Effie."

"Why? She'll be okay. Do you hear her when she's talking to you?"

"Of course! I'm not deaf!"

"Why don't you talk to her?"

"I don't want to give her false hope. I don't have much time left and she needs to be strong."

"She's a strong woman."

"I don't know what she'll do without me. She's never had to work. I've always taken care of her."

"How about your sons?"

"They both own their own businesses and have families of their own. Effie doesn't want to be a burden to them."

"She's their mother! They shouldn't look at taking care of her as a burden! She carried them in her body for nine months, wiped their butts and changed their diapers for many years. They should consider it a payback for services rendered."

"That's not how Effie sees it. She's old-fashioned and considers rearing a child to be a mother's maternal responsibility."

"I understand. Elton, roll over on your left side for me."

"Why? Are you going to poke me in the ass with a needle? I've had enough needles to last another lifetime."

"I'm not going to poke you with a needle. I want to listen to your lungs."

"What good will listening to my lungs do? I'm dying from brain cancer not lung cancer."

"I want to find out if your lungs are filling up with fluid."

"You don't have to listen to my lungs. I can tell you that they are. I can't take a deep breath."

"That's certainly an indication. Now roll over."

"No!"

"Elton, roll over or I'll order the nurses to give you an enema!"

"Okay! I'm rolling over. How's this?"

I placed the horn of my stethoscope in the middle of his back and listened intently to the 'swish' of blood pumping through his aorta and detected an erratic rhythm. His heart was failing.

"Okay doc what'd you hear?"

"Your lungs sound fine, but your heart is acting up. It won't be long now. Have you made your peace with Effie and your sons?"

Elton rolled back onto his back, smiled and looked me directly in the eye as he spoke. "I'm ready. Can you get this thing done before Effie comes back with that nosey nurse?"

"Are you certain that you're ready? Don't you want to tell Effie goodbye and that you love her?"

"She knows that! Come on Doc. Do whatever you have to do to get this over with!"

"Elton, I don't have to do anything. It's all up to you. Have you met Emma yet?"

"Emma? Do you mean that crazy old broad that dances around like she's a ballerina?"

"That's her."

"She came through here about a half hour ago and poked around."

"Did she open the window?"

"I don't think so. You can see it better than I can."

"It's not open. You're not ready to go."

"How do you know that I'm not ready to go? I want to go now! Let's do it!"

"If Emma was ready to show you the way out of here she would have opened the window for you. I think that she wants you to make peace with your wife and sons before she comes to get you."

"Why should that old broad have anything to do with my dying? I'm ready!"

"She died in Room 306 which is directly across the hall from here three years ago and there was no guide here to help her find her way out. The nurse on duty didn't know that she was supposed to open the window to allow her spirit to escape. So as a result, Emma's spirit is forever locked in the hospital. She came back to assume the responsibility of guiding patients through their window when it's time for them to go. She'll come and get you when she feels that you're ready."

"That's not fair!"

"Maybe it is and maybe it isn't, but when it's time for you to go she'll come for you."

"What if Emma doesn't come for me? I don't want to live like this!"

"Then maybe you'd better consider talking to Effie when she comes back and telling her how you feel about things. Emma has to take Effie's feeling into consideration as well. You might feel like you're alone in this transition, but you're not. Every member of your family plays a vital role in your passing. The sooner you make peace with all of them the sooner Emma will come for you."

"I see Emma! She's at the foot of my bed. Do you see her? She's finally come for me!"

"Now Elton, don't try to fool me. I know that Emma's not here. If she was I'd see her too."

"Okay. You caught me. Now what? Are you going to slap the back of my hands with a ruler?"

"I can't play any more games with you! I have to leave and see the rest of my patients before the shift change at seven o'clock. When Effie comes back and starts talking to you I want you to respond to her. She'll be thrilled."

"I don't want her to get her hopes up."

"She won't. She clearly understands your condition and what you're going through. That's why she went down to the nurses' station. The supervising nurse is briefing her as we speak on what to expect when you finally go."

"Won't that scare her?"

"No. Not a bit. Women understand the cycle of life much better than men do. She'll be okay."

"Elton, you've taken up enough of my time. Now I have to go and see the rest of the patients. Some of them are ready to go. I have to be there to evaluate their condition and give them the go ahead."

"I thought that was Emma's job."

"She does her thing from a subjective spiritual perspective. I do mine based on objective medical facts. I'll stop in see you tomorrow night."

"Do you really have to go? I'd like to talk with you some more. I changed my mind. I'm not ready to go just yet."

"Yes. I have to go. I told you that I have a lot more patients to see tonight."

"I'm going to take your advice and have a long talk with Effie when she comes back."

Goodbye Elton."

"Goodbye doctor."

I drifted out of the room into the wide hallway and paused to get my bearings. Emma was dipping and swirling her way down the hallway towards the nurses' station. She paused and stuck her tongue out at me. I knew that she was up to no good. I stuck my own tongue out as an immature response.

Elton's wife Effie was striding down the hall with a grim-faced Nurse Cathy in tow. The nurse did not look very happy and actually seemed to be fuming.

"Okay, Mrs. Klinger," the obviously highly irritated nurse hissed between her clenched teeth. "Your sons confirmed what you said. I'll shoot him up with eight milligrams of morphine and he'll go out like a light. You'll get a good night's sleep tonight."

"What if he wakes up and tries to talk?"

"He won't wake up tonight. I can guarantee that. We'll keep him knocked out with heavy doses of morphine and he won't feel any more pain before he finally goes."

"Some jokers apparently don't know when the jokes over," I mumbled to myself. *"No wonder Emma stuck her tongue out at me. I deserved it."*

I replaced the clipboard in the clear plastic holder beside the door and headed across the hall towards Room 306 and a new adventure.

Chapter
10

I paused in the hallway and turned to face the parking lot through the tinted plate glass window. I needed a few minutes to regain my senses and try to get a grip on reality. I've worked the night shift of this hospital for twenty-two years and for some reason I'm very tired tonight.

After I graduated from the University of Florida Medical School in Gainesville I spent three years as a resident at the Shands Teaching Hospital. After I completed my residency I accepted a job in the Emergency Room of the Port St. Lucie Medical Center, made it to Senior Resident, and never left.

Private practice was never one of my goals and I preferred to surround myself with the security of a corporation and be shielded from the day-to-day problems of running an office and dealing with a constant stream of patients. I must admit that being a resident physician has its ups and downs but in my mind it is heads and tails over private practice. I get a weekly paycheck right on schedule on Friday afternoon and don't have to worry about meeting a weekly payroll of my own, billing insurance companies and Medicare. Not to mention bottom-feeding lawyers and expensive malpractice suits.

I come on duty at eleven o'clock, complete my rounds in the Intensive Care Unit on the First Floor by twelve-thirty, pop up to the second floor, review each patient's file, stop by and visit with each patient, if they are awake, and try to finish by two o'clock. I habitually take a few minutes off for a cup of lukewarm coffee from the coffee machine on the first floor before I zip up to the third floor. The nurses are too busy to pay any attention to me as I review the patients' charts and make my rounds. I like the Third Floor the best because it's where I met Emma several years ago.

Emma and I developed a deep personal relationship over the two weeks that she spent on this floor three years ago. She had a severe case of chronic bronchial pneumonia and I couldn't find an antibiotic that would stop its deadly spread. Emma didn't have a chance and she knew it, but she put up a great fight. I was in her room holding her hand when she sat straight up in bed, ripped the oxygen mask off her face and bellowed out, "*I am woman! Hear me roar!*" She collapsed, took three deep breaths and stopped breathing. I considered attempting CPR, or even bringing in a crash cart equipped with a defibrillator, but decided against it. I knew that Emma didn't want to be brought back.

It was a very cold February night and the wind scraped against the window glass like a set of fingernails ripping across a slate chalkboard. Shortly after Emma took her last breath I heard a light tapping on the glass and walked over to the window to determine what was causing the irritating noise. I squinted through the tinted glass and saw a small twig lodged in the window frame that barely scraped the glass when a gust of wind caught it. I briefly thought about opening the window in an attempt to dislodge the twig, but reconsidered because of the cold. That mistake haunts me to this day.

The tiny twig scraping against the glass didn't cause the irritating tapping sound; it was Emma's guiding spirit outside the window desperately attempting to open the window so that Emma's own spirit could escape into the cold night air. I didn't learn until several hours later that the nurses automatically open the window immediately after death and by then it was too late. Emma's spirit was forever trapped in that room and would spend Eternity seeking out the spirits of dying patients in the hospital and leading them out an open window to freedom.

Emma doesn't let me forget my crucial oversight. She is always waiting for me when I get off the elevator on the third floor and she leads me on my nightly rounds. We have been working together for three years and she is a very important part of every patient's gentle death. Emma senses when a patient is ready to pass on and she guides them to the final result without uttering a word. If they are not ready, or have not made peace with their family, she holds them back for their own good. If a patient's spirit is not satisfied it might not ever leave the hospital and be destined to roam the halls much like Emma does. But, Emma doesn't need the competition!

I glanced at my wristwatch. It read four-seventeen. I've been on the third floor for two hours, have seen five patients and still have five patients to go. I always try to be done by six o'clock and that is coincidently the same time the cafeteria on the first floor opens for business. I want to get a hot cup of coffee and finish my paperwork by six forty-five because my shift ends at seven o'clock and I have to brief the morning staff on each patient's condition before I can clock out.

The visitors' parking lot is empty and the yellow street light globes cast an eerie pale light across the shiny asphalt. It wouldn't be long before the delivery vehicles will show up filled with fresh linens, food for the cafeteria and medical supplies. I often long for company on my rounds, but it would be very difficult for anyone to understand why I choose to make my rounds night after night. The nurses understand my methods and that it is best for them to ignore me as I go about my business. I stay out of their way and they stay out of mine. It makes for a good, but delicate relationship.

I heard a soft moan emanate from Room 306 that was directly behind me and to my left. I shrugged my shoulders, turned around and reached for the clipboard resting in the clear plastic holder mounted on the wall next to the door. Who was this patient and why did they need me tonight?

A ragged chill ran down my spine when I read the patient's name boldly printed on the top of the sheet of paper. The name was Lois Halfast! That was the name of a nurse who had worked with me on this floor for many years. I hoped against hope that it wasn't the Lois I knew! The chart indicated that she was a white female suffering from a terminal case of pancreatic cancer. She was fifty-five years old and not married. Sure sounds like my Lois!

Lois hated most men, including the doctors she was forced to work with on a day-to-day basis, but and only tolerated them. She would have been considered the Alpha female in an Alaskan wolf pack.

I was apprehensive and had no choice except to check on the patient. I tucked the clipboard under my left arm, took a deep breath and stepped through the open door.

Chapter
11

The patient appeared to be asleep. Her short salt and pepper, normally curly, short hair framed her bloated face much like an ancient gold leafed oaken frame would allow a Rembrandt to nestle between its arms without detracting from the beauty of the painting. It was my Lois and tonight she needed me!

Before I could take another step in her direction she appeared to sense my presence. Her eyes flickered and then opened wide as she spoke almost without moving her lips! "It's about time you got in here to see me! You've been poking around here and there and didn't even know that I was here!"

"Lois! Is that you?"

"Of course it is squirrel breath. Who were you expecting, the Virgin Mary perhaps? I'm sorry to disappoint you, but it's only me and I'm dying."

"I'm here now. Maybe I can help you," I sputtered as I slogged towards her bed. My feet felt like they were glued to the floor "No one told me that you were here. I'd have been here sooner if I had known."

"Look Doc. I wasn't an RN for thirty years for nothing. I know the score. They brought me in here yesterday to die."

"Don't give up hope. We might be able to control it with chemotherapy or radiation."

"I don't want either one of those things. The chemo kills as many good cells as it does bad ones and the radiation burns you up from the inside out. I'm ready to check out. I've got a one-. way ticket and its been punched by the man upstairs. He's calling me home."

"Don't talk like that!" I reached the side of Lois' bed and reached for her left hand. "Let me take your pulse."

"It wouldn't be a good reading. It went up twenty points when I saw you walk through the door."

"Come on Lois, behave yourself and let me take your pulse," I replied as I gently lifted her left arm and placed the tips of my fingers on the inside of her swollen wrist. "Do you have rheumatoid arthritis?"

"Of course. It runs in my family. There's no cartilage between my hand and wrist and it hurts like hell all the time."

"Have you tried taking Predizone? It's a strong steroid and will ease the pain."

"I tried it for awhile, but I bruised very badly if I bumped something."

"That's a normal side effect. Your pulse is seventy-eight beats per minute. That's normal."

"What did you expect? I'm not dead yet."

"You have lots of time left."

"Yeah. Right! Look doc, I know the score. When the pain gets too bad they're going to load me up with morphine and keep me in happy land until I go. That's okay with me. I'll be singing a happy tune on my way to the bone yard. I've been there and done that. I've seen a lot of patients die in thirty years of nursing and I used to work right here on this floor until I got really sick. I can stand the pain but I'm really afraid of dying. I don't know what happens after that. I don't want to die."

"Lois, no one wants to die, but it's not our choice. We can

only guess what happens afterwards. I think that it depends upon the person."

"Doctor, do you believe in ghosts?"

"I believe in restless spirits, but I have no opinion about ghosts."

"What's the difference between a restless spirit and a ghost?"

"A restless spirit is the soul of a person that cannot rest because they never finished the work they were supposed to complete before they passed on. A ghost is the spirit of a person who died in a tragic way and cannot rest because of the way they died. Many restless spirits serve as guardians of the place where they died and protect others from harm."

"Doc, do you remember a woman named Emma? She died in this room three years ago and she roams the halls every night."

"Yes. I remember Emma."

"I was holding her hand when she slipped away, but I didn't know that I was supposed to open the window to let her spirit escape the hospital. She's comes back here every night to remind me that I screwed up. Did you see her tonight?"

"Yes. I saw her out in the hall a few minutes ago. I thought she was on the way in to see you."

"Did she say anything to you?"

"She blew me a kiss."

"Weren't you in her room too when she passed?"

"Yes. I was. I was standing right beside you."

"Did you know about opening the window?"

"No. I didn't. That's a relatively new superstition, but Emma pops in every night when I'm coming through on my rounds."

"Do you think that anyone else besides you and me sees her?"

"I'm not sure. But the nurses all know that she comes through every night."

"What makes you say that?"

"When I got off the elevator I heard one of them mention that Emma was here."

"Oh."

"Lois, I never got to know you very well when you were working here in the hospital. Would you mind telling me a little about yourself?"

"What do you want to know?"

"Where were you born?"

"Corry, Pennsylvania. It's a quiet factory town of about ten thousand people about twenty miles southeast of Erie."

"I know where Corry is. I've been there."

"Why would you go to a little berg like Corry?"

"It's a long story and I don't have time to tell it tonight."

"Come on doctor. You can tell me."

"Okay. My aunt and uncle lived in Buffalo, New York and they had a small cottage on Canadohta Lake. I used to spend time there during the summer. They're both gone."

"Doc, is your family originally from Buffalo?"

"Lois, let's talk about you. Where did you go to school?"

"I graduated from Corry High School and went to Penn State for four years."

"Did you graduate?"

"I just told you that I was there for four years. That normally indicates that a person graduated."

"Not always. Some students attend college for more than four years and don't graduate."

"I've seen some of them. They'll stay in school as long as their mommy and daddy keep paying their tuition."

"I know a few of those myself. How much do you know about your condition? What have the doctors told you?"

"I'm at the end stage of pancreatic cancer. It's metastasized into my lungs, liver and bladder. They haven't told me if it reached my brain yet, but I'm sure it has."

"Have they done an MRI?"

"Yes. But the radiologist hasn't told me what he found. But, it's no big deal. I'm ready."

"What did you mean by that? What are you ready for?"

"I'm ready to die provided that I can do it without pain. You made me feel comfortable about going."

"How did I do that?"

"Just by being here and talking with me. Emma stuck her head in the door a minute ago and gave me a 'thumbs up'. It must be time for me to go. Tell those lazy nurses to get their butts in here and get me on a heavy morphine drip before I change my mind."

"Lois, I'm not your primary care physician. I can't order them to do anything."

"You've been in this hospital for a long time. I remember you making late night rounds way back when I first started working here. You've got a lot of pull. Please, do it as a favor to me."

"I'll see what I can do."

"Will you open the window for me?"

"It's already open. Emma opened it when she came through here a few minutes ago. She's waiting for you outside. Don't be afraid. She'll show you the way."

"Thank you doctor. I'm looking forward to seeing you on the other side. You'll need a good nurse."

"I'm expecting it. You're the best of the best."

"Thank you for the compliment."

"You're very welcome. Have a good trip and don't be afraid."

"I'm not afraid any more."

"Good. I'll see you on the other side."

"How about if I come back and work with you and Emma?"

"That's fine with me if you can find a way to do it."

"Do you think that Emma will be jealous?"

"Why should she be jealous?"

"She's had you all to herself for the last three years."

"Emma's not a nurse and you are. There's plenty of room in this hospital for both of you."

"Thank you doctor. I'm almost ready to go. Will you ask the senior RN to come in and start a heavy morphine drip for me so I can check out without pain? I'd like to be smiling when I leave."

"Yes. I will. Goodbye Lois." I rose to leave and winked at her with my right eye. "Have a safe trip."

"Good-bye doc. I'll see you very soon."

"I'll be waiting right here for you." I turned and left the room as I wiped the tears from my cheeks with my right hand. It was going to be a very long night.

Chapter
12

I paused outside of Lois' room and paused to listen to two nurses, Hazel and the rookie Debbie, talking in the hall while they were preparing the medications cart.

"I heard her talking to somebody," Debbie whispered to Hazel. The young Phillipino nurse wasn't certain if Hazel and Marilyn were messing with her earlier, or if the story of Emma's spirit roaming the hospital was true. "There's somebody in there with her."

"She must have been talking to Emma," Hazel grimly replied. "She's on the floor tonight. I saw her come off the elevator."

"She's a ghost! How could you see her?"

"I didn't see her in person. I saw the elevator door open about a quarter after one and it was empty. Everyone knows that's when Emma shows up."

"I don't believe in ghosts!"

"Emma's not a ghost. She's a spirit."

"Why is she here? Is she trying to scare the patients to death?"

"Just the opposite. She's here to help the patients gently pass away without fear or pain."

"Why?"

"Emma died in Room 306 three years ago. The duty nurse didn't know that she was supposed to open the window and let Emma's spirit out. So, Emma's spirit roams the hall every night opening the window for patients who are ready to go."

"That's a bunch of crap! I don't believe it. You're just trying to scare me because I'm new here and I don't scare easily!"

"You don't? Then who do you think opened the window?"

"It was closed when I checked on her at one-thirty!"

"If I didn't open it and you didn't open it who did? The tooth fairy?"

"Maybe the night shift doctor did when he was making his rounds?"

"He wouldn't make the effort. Emma opened it and that's who the patient was talking to."

"She's been out cold since we came on duty at seven. I think that she was having an endorphin rush and talking to the television set. The nurse I relieved told me that she had an endorphin rush about four o'clock yesterday afternoon and was blabbering away to anyone who would listen to her."

"Debbie, you're a sweet girl, and you can believe whatever you want. Are you ready to go in and check her vitals? Her chart has to be up to date when she passes or our butts will be in a sling for sure."

The skeptical young nurse peeked into the open doorway, turned back and whispered, "The television set isn't on."

"I told you! Emma probably turned it off when she came in and talked to her."

"You freak me out!"

"Silly girl! How can she not believe in Emma?" I chuckled to myself as I made a few notes on my clipboard. *"I saw her myself and even I don't believe in spirits."*

Chapter
13

Certainly by now you realize that Emma and I enjoy an unusual working relationship by any standard. She goes about doing her thing and I do mine. She stays out of my way and I do my best to stay out of hers. It's not often that a physician gets to share his late night rounds with a restless spirit.

Emma doesn't bother me, but sometimes she makes herself a little too obvious. The nurses know that she's there, but then again they don't want to believe that she's there. Does that make sense to you? Everyone wants to believe that there is something after death, after all immortality is what writers strive to achieve. Their physical being may be gone from this dimension, but their published works live forever, provided that someone reads them.

The fear of absolute nothingness is what terminal patients fear the most. The final act of death seems to be so final as it were and they wonder what's beyond Death's open door. We will all find out what's behind that door one day, but the circumstances will most likely be out of our control and that lack of final control is what terrifies us. I have seen the black mask of death fall over the faces of many patients and none of them could push it off.

After visiting with Lois and escaping into the safety of the hallway I glanced at my watch. It read a pitiful 4:57 A.M. It was almost five o'clock and I spent forty minutes in Lois' room. I couldn't spare that much time for each of the four remaining patients! I wanted to be done with my rounds and in the hospital cafeteria by six o'clock for a cup of hot coffee.

"If I spend fifteen minutes with each of the remaining four patients I can be done with my rounds by six o'clock and sipping fresh, hot coffee in the cafeteria," I thought to myself. *"I'd better get my butt in gear and stop yakking with the patients."*

I looked up, caught a movement out of the corner of my right eye and swung my head in that direction. Emma was standing on her head in the center of the hallway and using her extended arms to form a tripod with her hands. She stuck her tongue out at me, flipped to an upright stance and skipped down the hall towards the nurses' station.

"Oh no Emma!" I mumbled out loud. *"Leave them alone!"* Fortunately I caught myself before I said another word. Two nurses, Debbie the young Phillipino nurse and Cathy an experienced LPN, were standing less than three feet away from me and reviewing Lois medications on the computer.

"Hazel, did you say something about Emma?" Debbie asked.

"What?" Hazel responded as she turned to face Debbie. "Why would I say anything about Emma?"

"I thought I heard you call out to her."

"I didn't, but what do you think you heard me say?"

"I thought you said something about leaving them alone."

"Leaving who alone?"

"Maybe us?"

"Why would I say that if I was standing here right beside you?"

"I don't know. But your voice sounded a little masculine."

"Shut up! It's not my fault. My voice changed after I went through menopause! Let's get in there and shoot Lois up. I worked with her for almost twenty years and she'd do the same for me."

"How much morphine are you going to give her?"

"The doctor authorized four milligrams every three hours, but I have a little extra and I'm going to give her eight milligrams."

"How did you get extra morphine?"

"Hazel, how long have you worked in a hospital as a nurse?"

"Two weeks. This is my first job."

"Let me help you understand something. When a doctor prescribes four milligrams every three hours that's the maximum we are supposed to give the patient. However, some patients need less than what the doctor prescribed to kill their pain. But then again, others may need more. So, an experienced nurse experiments here and there with the dosage."

"I don't understand."

"I start out by giving a patient two milligrams of morphine every three hours. If that works I'm two milligrams ahead of the game every two hours, that's sixteen milligrams at the end of a shift, and I can administer it to any patient who needs it to kill their pain."

"Doesn't the computer measure and record the dosage when you scan the patient's wristband?"

"All that stupid machine knows is that the doctor prescribed four milligrams and it spit out four milligrams. It doesn't know if we injected two or four milligrams. It's simple."

"What if the doctor finds out?"

"How can he find out?"

"If he prescribed four milligrams and it doesn't stop the patient's pain won't he be suspicious?"

"No. He'll increase the dosage to six milligrams and I'll give the patient four. The patient's pain will go away and I'm still two milligrams ahead. It's fool proof."

"Isn't that illegal?"

"So is jaywalking and cheating on your income taxes, but whose telling?"

"I won't tell anyone. What do you do with the extra morphine if you don't use it up during your shift?"

"I take it home and use it to relax me before I go to sleep. It's great stuff! You should try it if you're keyed up after a shift."

"Isn't morphine addictive?"

"Maybe, but who cares? You only live once. Are you ready to get in there and help Lois shoot up?"

"I suppose. What if she doesn't need all eight milligrams?"

"She needs all of it and probably even more. We all agreed to help her out of this mess."

"What do you mean?"

"Do you need a roadmap for everything? All of the nurses on this shift agreed to hold back two milligrams of morphine from each one of their patients. It's five o'clock now and we'll give her eight milligrams, another eight at six o'clock, eight more at six-thirty and another eight just before shift change at seven. She'll be gone by seven-thirty."

"Are you deliberately overdosing the patient? You'll shut down her respiration. That's euthanasia! It's against the law."

"Who says it's overdosing? We only gave her the prescribed dosage of four milligrams every three hours. You can check the computer if you like."

"I don't know if I want to be a part of this!"

"Do you want to go home at seven o'clock?"

"Of course. Why?"

"Eight milligrams of morphine will put anyone down for three hours. It could be that you became addicted to morphine in nursing school, snuck off into a storage closet to shoot up and overdosed. You are young and pretty to boot. That would be a real shame."

"I don't take drugs!"

"Maybe you do, and maybe you don't, but you had better figure out how things work around here real quick or the next shift might find you in a closet with a big smile on your face."

"I understand. I'm ready," the naïve young nurse responded and formed a circle with her right thumb and forefinger. "Let's get in there and put Lois in Happy Land."

After the two nurses entered Lois' room I directed my attention to reading the chart of the patient in Room 307.

Tommy Hall is an energetic nine-year old black youngster who loves to play Little League baseball. He's big for his age at five foot seven inches tall, plays third base with a vengeance and was on the St. Lucie County All Star team for the last two seasons. He dreams of playing third base in the Little League World Series in McKeesport, Pennsylvania and attending Florida State on a baseball scholarship. After graduation from college he has ambitions of playing for the Florida Marlins.

According to his chart Tommy has a very big problem. His right leg snapped just above the knee when he slid into third base during an All Star game. An orthopedic surgeon found that the tibia was eaten clear through by an aggressive cancer and amputated Tommy's right leg at the hip. A CT Scan revealed that the cancer has spread to his spine.

Tommy constantly cries out for his family. They aren't there to comfort him because they have no way to get to the hospital.

Tommy's father worked as a groundskeeper at Mets stadium in Port St. Lucie until he broke his back when he fell into a dugout. He is paralyzed from the waist down, confined to a wheelchair and cannot drive a car because he can't afford to have the necessary equipment installed on it. He played semi-pro baseball in a black sandlot league for three years and had the chance to go with a major league farm team. But he couldn't leave Fort Pierce because he had to take care of his mother, five brothers and three sisters. Tommy's mother is disabled with severe glaucoma and can't drive a car. Her doctors predict that she will be totally blind within six months.

Tommy is the oldest sibling and has three younger brothers and two younger sisters. They are all counting on him making it big in professional baseball.

According to the notes in his chart no one has told Tommy that his right leg is gone!

I looked around the hallway for moral support and Emma was nowhere in sight. I was on my own this time. *"Why does it always have to be me?"* I muttered as I entered the darkened room.

Chapter 14

"*Why does it always have to be me?*" I repeated under my breath as I walked to nine year-old Tommy Hall's bedside. He opened his eyes and looked up at me with Cocker Spaniel eyes. It was clear that he didn't know.

"Hello Mr. Doctor," Tommy bubbled. "I've been waiting for you to come and see me."

"You have?" I cautiously responded. "How did you know I was coming to see you tonight?"

"Miss Emma told me. She played checkers with me and I beat her good."

"She beats me most of the time. I think she cheats."

"Mr. Doctor would you please scratch my right leg for me? It itches like crazy just above my knee, but I can't reach it. They've got this big tent over my legs and I can't get my hand under it."

"*Oh God!*" I silently screamed to myself. "*What have you gotten me into this time? What have I done to be punished so severely? I can't do this.*" Then I realized that I must. I had no choice. I mustered the meager mental strength that remained and pushed my right hand under the tent covering, felt for a leg, found one and scratched it above the knee. "How's that?" I cautiously inquired.

"That's my left knee. Scratch the right one, please." Tommy smiled liked an innocent cherub featured in a Reuben's' Renaissance painting.

"Tommy, did you know that you hurt your leg really bad when you slid into third base?"

"I felt it twist when my foot hit the bag, but the umpire called me safe! I don't remember very much after that."

"Yes, you were called safe, but you injured your right leg very badly. You had to have surgery on your leg to repair it and the best doctors in the hospital worked on you."

"Did they fix it? I'm going to play in the Little League World Series in McKeesport, Pennsylvania this summer if we win the state championship!"

"Tommy, the surgeons had to remove your leg."

"That's okay, I guess. Can you sew on another one?"

"No, Tommy we can't sew on another one."

"Will it grow back like a frog's leg? 1 had a pet frog called Herman. Our cat ate his right leg and it grew back in two weeks."

"Herman was an amphibian and they can grow back legs. Humans are mammals and we can't. When your hip heals you will be fitted with an artificial leg. We call it a prosthetic limb."

"Can I still play baseball?"

"Maybe after rehabilitation. You'll have to learn how you walk and run with the prosthesis."

"Will I be able to run good enough to be on the All Star team? They really need me at third base."

"I don't know. It will be up to you as how well you adapt to the prosthesis."

"I'll bet that some professional baseball players have artificial legs. Some of them run kinda funny."

"I'll bet they do too. Tommy, what's your favorite movie?"

"*The Field of Dreams.* I liked seeing the old time baseball players and the way they disappeared into the cornfield. Did you know that they were really ghosts?"

"They were spirits not ghosts."

"What's the difference?"

"A spirit is the restless image of a person who didn't finish something that was very important to him when they were alive. They won't hurt you. Most spirits are very friendly. Miss Emma is a spirit."

"I like Miss Emma. She opened the window for me."

"Tommy, would you like to play baseball with the old time baseball players in the same cornfield that you saw in *The Field of Dreams*?"

"Yes! When I can I start?"

"You'll have to ask Miss Emma when she comes back to check on you later. I think that you'll be back playing baseball with both legs very soon with famous baseball players like Babe Ruth, Shoeless Joe Jackson, Mickey Mantle and Ted Williams. Would you like that?"

"Yes! But I don't understand. How can I do that if I'm in the hospital?"

"You will being playing baseball at *The Field of Dreams* very soon."

"Can my mommy, daddy, brothers and sisters come to watch me play?"

"Of course," I lied.

There was no response. Tommy's eyes were closed and the white sheet was moving where his right leg used to be. I felt someone watching me and glanced around the room. Emma was standing beside the open window and waving goodbye to someone outside.

"*Have a great game Tommy and be careful the next time you slide into third base,*" I whispered.

"I will Mr. Doctor," came a soft response from the still figure. Tommy's lips didn't move!

I took a deep breath, softly patted the young boy on the forehead, turned towards the open doorway and caught a glimpse of a sheet-covered gurney, pushed by two male attendants, leaving Lois' room.

"*Emma, thank you for opening the window for him,*" I softly muttered under my breath. *"I would hate for that young boy to wind up wandering the halls of this hospital for eternity. It's bad enough to see you every night when I'm making my rounds."*

"You're very welcome doctor," a soft feminine voice whispered in my left ear. Her voice made no sound and felt like a light spring breeze skipping across a still pond. "It's my job."

Chapter
15

I slowly drifted out of Tommy's room and headed for the quiet hallway. The sheet-covered gurney and the two attendants disappeared inside the service elevator as the polished aluminum doors silently squeezed shut behind them. Lois was in a better place. Life was over for her, but my shift still had time left on the clock. The oval-faced wall clock at the end of the hallway read 5:22. I still had to see three more patients, write up my report and find a hot cup of coffee in the cafeteria.

The graveyard shift was no fun and was usually the break-in shift for new residents. I preferred the quietness of the night and lack of visitors when I made my rounds. The patients tend to open up to me when there is no one else around to overhear our conversation, except when Emma sticks her big nose in my business! But, she's been here for three years and from what I see she has no intention of giving up her post unless a spirit with more seniority comes along and bumps her out. I wonder who makes the decision for a spirit shift change? Does God do it or is the decision delegated to a lowly subordinate? Perhaps there's a Director of Spirit Human Resources roaming the broad halls of the 'Hereafter' and making job assignments. I wonder where Emma would go next? I've gotten used to seeing her every night and so have the nurses. It would be hard to convince them that Emma was reassigned and that they have to break in a new spirit guide on the proper way to open the window for the spirit of a dying patient. Maybe it's time for Emma to retire.

"*I'm not ever going to retire,*" whispered a light female voice somewhere deep in my brain. "*And neither are you. We're in this thing together Mr. Doctor. You talk to them, make them feel warm and fuzzy all over and I shove them out of the window when it's time for them to hit the road. It's a good system and the folks in Spirit Resources gave me an 'Outstanding' rating last quarter. I was the only spirit guide in this county to receive an 'Outstanding' rating.*"

"So, what do you want from me Emma?" I responded out loud. "Do you want a pat on the back from me too? You're apt to break your arm if you keep patting yourself on the back. Just do your job."

"*Well! You don't have to get so huffy about it!*" The soft female voice responded. "*I was just simply pointing out to you that the 'powers that be' think a lot of me.*"

"What about the patients?" I quipped. You're shoving them out the window so fast that they don't have time to consider the alterative of staying around here just a little while longer."

"*There's a premium on bed space in this hospital if you hadn't noticed! Patients are coming through the Emergency Room and into Intensive Care faster than I can move them through here!*"

"Are you on a quota? Do you get a bonus at the end of the fiscal year, and a trip to Cancun, Mexico during Spring Break, if you exceed your quota of freed spirits?"

"*No! I'm not on a quota. What I do is a matter of basic math. There are ten rooms in this wing and they are reserved for terminal patients who have declined artificial life support. There are ten beds in Intensive Care and ten beds in the Emergency Room. The Emergency Room can't transfer a patient to the*

Intensive Care Unit until the ICU frees up a bed. There's only two ways to do that."

"What does that have to do with you?"

"I move a few of them out the Emergency Room in order to keep the ICU from backing up. If there are no rooms available up here they can't transfer any patients up from ICU, so I also thin out the ICU as best I can."

"Emma! What are you saying?"

"I'm kind of like a Triage Unit. I evaluate the patients for transfer to the other side. Those who have found peace within themselves and with their loved ones go first. Those patients who have some unfulfilled need, or need more time to make peace with their family, are given a little more time."

"Are you the Angel of Death?"

"Of course not! That clown runs around dressed up in that stupid-looking black cape and whipping around that rusty scythe. It's dull as a rock and it couldn't cut melted butter. He has a lousy bedside manner and he scares people. You haven't seen that sneak around here have you?"

"No. Should I be looking for him?"

"No. He doesn't have any interest in you, or me either. The Director of Spirit Resources ordered him to stay out of my territory. If he shows up in this hospital I'll kick his butt and he knows it! I studied King Fu when I was assigned to the Beijing Hospital. I tangled with him once in San Francisco over a young girl with brain cancer. After that little charade he was assigned to the prison on Alcatraz Island for ninety days."

"What? A spirit was sent to Alcatraz? What did he do there? Rot away in a cell?"

"He wasn't sent there as a prisoner. He was supposed to terrorize the prisoners on Death Row and from what I hear he did it very well. Three Lifers died from heart attacks the first week he was there. He thinned out the ranks and freed up lots of cells for fresh inmates from the mainland."

"Emma, let's go back to your perceived role in this hospital. So, what you're telling me is that you make the decision as to whether a patient lives or dies?"

"No. I make a recommendation as to when, not if, and only

after I make an objective evaluation of the patient's physical and mental condition, ascertain if his, or her, affairs are in order and if they have made peace with their family members. If everything checks out that's when they check out."

"So, whatever medical evaluation that I, or any other physician makes, is irrelevant as far as you're concerned?"

"That's correct."

"Then what I am I doing here?"

"A very good job, even if I do say so myself."

"But what good am I doing if my decisions have nothing to do with whether the patient lives or dies? I feel useless."

"You are doing a lot of good! You are helping patients to find inner peace before they check out. Your efforts, and the patient's reaction to you, are a vital part of my evaluation. I'm always watching you and I listen very carefully to how you react with the patients. You have an excellent bedside manner. If I was your supervisor I'd give you an 'Outstanding' rating."

"Thank goodness you're not my supervisor. I still have three patients to see before shift change at seven o'clock."

"I think that you're looking forward to having a hot cup of coffee when the cafeteria opens at six o'clock."

"What makes you think that?"

"I'm a spirit and I can read your thoughts like a primary school reader. I'm inside your head talking to you right now. But, you look kind of silly standing out here in the hallway talking to yourself. No one can hear me except you. If someone sees you out here talking to yourself you are apt to be taken away for a psychiatric evaluation."

"Don't you have something else to do besides harass me? I still have patients to see tonight."

"I do too. I'll be right ahead of you. Watch for me."

"Why don't you leave them alone? You've freed up enough beds tonight!"

"There was a multi-car accident on the Florida Turnpike out by Yee Haw Junction about an hour ago and the Emergency Room is flooded with Trauma Patients. So is the Fort Pierce Hospital. I have to open up some beds so they can transfer patients up here from ICU stat!"

"Why don't you make a detour down to the Emergency Room and ICU first?"

"That's a good idea. Do you think you can handle the last three patients all by yourself? I've already checked them out."

"That really makes me feel like a one-armed paper hanger. If you've already been in to see them then you know which ones are going to live or die tonight. I might as well quit for the night."

"Don't be that way! I haven't made my final decision. I'll take your input into consideration as part of my evaluation. But don't pout if everything doesn't come out the way you want it to."

"How can you take my input into consideration if you're going to be in the ER and ICU?"

"I'm in your head. Don't you remember? I see and hear everything that you do. Doc, I've got to be going. I'll catch up with you later."

Just down the hall from where I stood with my back against the wall the elevator door silently glided opened and closed. No one got on, or off, the elevator. The nurses all knew who it was.

I glanced at the wall clock. It read 5:33. I didn't have much time left to complete my rounds. I had to get going! I turned to my right, took three steps, reached the door to Room 308, removed the clipboard from the clear plastic holder, scanned the patient's summary sheet and read it to myself.

"The patient, Libby McGraw, is a white female, age thirteen, diagnosed with Stage Four retinal eye cancer in both eyes. The virulent cancer has metastasized to her brain and a surgical team from Miami removed both of her eyes yesterday afternoon."

I replaced the clipboard into its holder, took a deep breath and cautiously slipped silently through the door. Emma's soft voice simultaneously echoed in my brain. *"Be very quiet. Libby's parents, her older sister Dawn age sixteen, and her younger brother Josh, age nine, have been sitting by her bedside since she came out of the Recovery Room. Libby's heavily sedated and doesn't know that her family is with her. She's not expected to last until dawn. Be gentle, do what you have to do and leave."* I nodded my head in quiet acknowledgement of her message.

"I don't want to be here!" My brain screamed as my eyes scanned the darkened room.

Chapter
16

Libby's mother Terry is sitting on the edge of her chair between Libby's bed and the window. Her father is sitting in a chair between the door and Libby's bed. Libby's older sister Dawn is standing at the foot of the bed staring down at her younger sister's unconscious body. Her younger brother Josh doesn't understand what's going on and is intently concentrating on playing a basketball video game on his Play Master hand-held video controller.

Libby's mother is holding Libby's limp hand and urging her to go and see her grandpa and grandma both of whom died from carbon monoxide poisoning in their home two years earlier. Her grandfather purchased a kerosene room heater and set it up in the living room on an extremely cold January night. All of the windows were closed tight and sealed with plastic sheeting and duct tape to prevent air leaks. It also prevented the carbon monoxide from escaping. The geriatric couple smothered to death during the night and Libby's mother found them the next morning when she came to the house to check on why her mother didn't answer the telephone.

"Libby sweetheart. It's okay. You can go now. Grandma and grandpa are waiting for you on the other side. It's a much better place. There's no pain there and you will be able to see with both eyes," she whispered as she softly squeezed the unconscious girl's right hand. "If you can hear me squeeze my hand."

"Did she squeeze back?" Asked Libby's father. "I'm holding her left hand and I think I felt something."

"No. Nothing," the anxious mother responded. I don't think she hears us."

"One of the nurses told me that unconscious people can hear everything we say," chimed in Dawn. "They may not be able to physically respond, but she said they can hear us."

"Don't refer to your sister as they!" Libby's mother snapped back. "Her name is Elizabeth!"

"Okay mom, whatever."

"Josh! What are you doing?" His mother snapped. "Come over here and talk to your sister."

"What good will that do? She's unconscious. Besides I'm playing video basketball."

"Richard! Tell your son to turn off that damn video game and talk to his sister!"

"Terry you know in your heart that Libby's out of it. She's not ever going to wake up. The doctor said that the CT Scan showed that the cancer is in her brain. Let him be."

There wasn't anything that I could offer the family in the way of a favorable prognosis or solace. I decided to just stand in the doorway and quietly observe them.

"Hey doc! Do you want to know about the family?" Emma's voice teased my brain.

"Emma! What are you doing here?" I thought. I knew that she could hear me because we communicate telepathically. *"Can't you leave this girl alone? Aren't you supposed to be in the Emergency Room and ICU clearing out bed space?"*

"I'm still in ICU. I picked up your concern and thought that you might like an update."

"What do you want to tell me?"

"Do you want to know about her parents? It might help you later."

"Sure. Why not!" I thought. *"Make it short. This girl doesn't have much time left."*

"She has as much time as we give her."

"What do you mean by that?" I felt silly thinking that I was having a mental conversation with a spirit. I must be having delusions. *"You've made all of the life and death decisions tonight!"*

"She needs to talk to you before she goes. The window isn't open is it?"

"No, it's not. How can she talk to me if she's unconscious? Her parents will flip out if she wakes up and starts talking to me!"

"Don't worry about her parents."

"What do you mean don't worry about her parents? They're a big part of this!"

"They're going to leave for awhile and you can talk to her while they're gone."

"Where're they going?"

"Over to the Denny's on Federal Highway for breakfast. The mother works there as a waitress. She can rap with her friends and they'll give her some moral support."

"What about her brother and sister?"

"They're going too."

"What does the father do for a living?"

"He works in a bait and tackle shop over in Jensen Beach."

"Are Libby and her sister close?"

"Not really. There're too many years between them. Libby's thirteen years old and her sister's seventeen and captain of the cheerleading squad at Port Saint Lucie High School. She considerers Libby to be a pest because she listens on her telephone calls and sneaking peeks at her diary."

"What about the brother?"

"Josh is even a bigger pest and bugs both girls. He doesn't

quite understand what's happening to Libby and he's better off playing video games. His mother keeps telling him to put it away and talk to his sister, but he thinks it's a waste of time because she doesn't talk back."

"What do you want me to do?"

"Since when does a spirit tell a doctor what to do? I don't have a medical degree."

"You've been doing it all night!"

"No I haven't! I just determine if they're ready to go and I facilitate their departure. It's your job to do tests, examine them and prescribe treatment."

"I haven't been able to do that tonight because you've sent them all out the window!"

"I had to free up some beds. There's going to be a really big accident on Port St. Lucie Boulevard during the early morning rush hour and the Emergency Room's going to be swamped."

"How do you know that?"

"It's my job. I'm a spirit and I can see into the future."

"What time is the accident going to happen and exactly where on Port St. Lucie Boulevard?"

"Do you know where the Rivergate Shopping Plaza is on Port St. Lucie Boulevard?"

"Of course. It's a couple blocks past the People's Bank on the corner of Holland Street."

"That's where it's going to happen at exactly seven twenty-four."

"Now you're stretching it!"

"No I'm not. A big truck is going to pull out of the parking lot onto Port St. Lucie Boulevard and a school bus loaded with grade school children is going to slam into it. It isn't going to be pretty."

"How many of those innocent kids are you going to wipe out?"

"It won't be my decision. I get off at seven o'clock. Someone else will be filling in here."

"Who is it? Maybe I'll stay around and help them."

"You don't know her. Besides, I'm the only spirit that you're programmed to see."

"This is crazy! I must be having delusions. I must be working

too many hours."

"I think so. You've been working the shift every night for the past week. You need some time off. Maybe you can find someone to fill in for you tomorrow night?"

"No! I'm the only doctor that has worked the night shift for twenty-two years!!"

"Then cool it and talk to the girl. I'll hustle her family out of the room."

"How can you do that? They can't see or hear you!"

"I'm a good spirit and I can do anything. Just watch me."

"Terry sweetheart," Libby's father addressed her mother. "Let's take a break and go over to Denny's for breakfast. You can fill the girls in on her condition."

"What about Libby!" She responded with a startled look on her face. "She needs us!"

"She'll be just fine and she'll wait for us to come back."

"Maybe not Dad," Dawn retorted. "One of the nurses told me that quite often a patient will not die until all of the family members have left the room. They don't want the family to be embarrassed by watching them die."

"Dawn! Show some respect for your sister," he retorted. "She'll hang on as long as she wants and when she's ready she'll pass."

"Whatever," Dawn replied and blew a big, pink bubble. "I'm just passing along what a nurse told me." The pale pink bubble popped and spread pink bubble gum all over her face.

"That's your sister's spirit getting even with you for saying that," her mother retorted. "It's a little stuffy in here. I'm going to open the window a crack before we leave. Maybe some fresh air will be good for her."

"No! Don't open the window!" I screamed in my mind, but she paid no attention to my plea. It was not my place to interfere in family matters. *"Emma must have had something to do with this!"*

"No I didn't," I distinctly heard in my brain. *"I'm still in the ICU. I think the mother knows."*

The mother reached for the window crank and turned it until there was a four-inch gap between the window and the frame.

"That should do it. Let's go have breakfast."

The father motioned for Josh and Dawn to leave the room and waited for his wife to come around the end of Libby's bed and stand beside him. He put his left arm around her waist and whispered in her ear. "I think that you did the right thing. It's best for us to leave for a while and allow Libby to decide what's best for her. If she wants to pass while we're gone it's her decision."

"I agree, but it's hard for a mother to leave her dying child. I'm going to miss her."

"I'm going to miss her too. She has the best doctors in the county looking after her. It's just about time for one of them to come through on his rounds."

I stepped out into the hall to allow the anxious couple to walk out of the room without me getting in their way. They paid no attention to me and said nothing as they walked past. I waited until I saw the elevator doors close behind them before I re-entered Libby's room.

Libby was sitting up in bed and smiling when I walked in.

"It took them long enough to leave didn't it?" She remarked. "Doctor I think that I'm ready to go but I don't want to die in front of my parents. That would be embarrassing for them and me too. Yuk! Tell my sister that she was right. I heard everything. I'm going to come back as a ghost and hide out under my brother's bed. I'm to going to haunt the hell out of that little bastard until he leaves home."

"I understand Libby. How do you feel?"

"I feel fine but I can't see anything with these bandages over my eyes. Can you take them off so I can see you?"

"Don't you know about your eyes?"

"Sure Do! My boyfriend told me that they're as blue as the center of the Gulf Stream and sparkle brighter than the brightest blue star sapphire."

"I'm certain of that. Did you know that you have retinal cancer in both eyes?"

"That's old news!"

"The surgeons removed both of your eyes yesterday afternoon. That's why you can't see me."

"Why don't you humor me and take off the bandages? Please?"

"If you insist, but I don't want you to be disappointed if you can't see me."

"I can see you right now. I want you to take off the bandages so you look into my eyes before I go."

"But Libby, you don't have any eyes! The surgeons removed them yesterday."

"You might be surprised. Will you please take off the bandages?"

"Okay. If that's what you want," I replied as I moved to the side of her bed and removed the angel-wing clip holding the outer heavy gauze warping in place.

"That's what I want."

"Let me know if it hurts you and I'll stop."

"It won't hurt. I'm way past pain. How did my mother know to open the window for me?"

"What do you mean?"

"Who told her to open the window so my spirit could escape the hospital?"

"I don't know what you mean by that?"

"Haven't you worked in this hospital for a long time?"

"Yes. I've been here for twenty-two years."

"Then you should know that all of the nurses are told to open a window before a patient dies so their spirit can escape and not be trapped in here. Emma's a trapped spirit."

"How do you know about Emma?"

"She stopped by my room and talked to me just before you came in."

"Emma! You sneak!" I said out loud. "You double-crossed me!"

"No I didn't," Emma replied directly into my brain. *"It was Libby's choice and her mother made the final decision. One of her mother's friends is a nurse and she told her what to do."*

"Is she on this floor? I'll have her mangy hide nailed to the wall for interfering with my patient!"

"No. She works in Martin Memorial Hospital North in Stuart and you can't touch her. Now help Libby with her bandages! She

wants you to see her pretty blue eyes before she goes."

"But Libby's eyes were surgically removed yesterday afternoon according to her chart!"

"*Charts can be wrong. Nurses, and even doctors, make mistakes once in a while. Doctor, do you believe in miracles?*"

"No! I believe in medical facts!"

"*Then finish removing her bandages.*"

"I don't think I can. I don't want to see what's under them."

"*You don't have any choice. She wants you to see her blue eyes before she goes.*"

"What about her family?"

"*What about them?*"

"If her eyes are still there wouldn't they want to see them too?"

"*Don't act stupid! Just take off the girl's bandages before I come up there and do it for you!*"

"Doctor, who are you talking to about me?" Libby innocently asked. "There's nobody here except you and me."

"I was talking to Emma," I timidly responded as I unwound the final layer of white gauze to expose her empty eye sockets. They were packed with white gauze. "How do you know there's nobody here besides us?"

"I looked! How do my eyes look to you doctor?"

"They are as deep a blue as the center of the Gulf Stream and sparkle brighter than the brightest blue star sapphire."

"I knew that you would say that when you saw them," Libby replied as she closed her empty eye sockets, sighed and sank back into the depths of her pillow.

A saw a bright flicker of blue light outside the window as I hurriedly replaced the multi-layered gauze wrapping around Libby's head and eyes. I thought I heard voices in the hall. It was Libby's family returning from Denny's! I snapped the angel-wing clip in place and slipped into the bathroom. It was better that they didn't see me, or know about my conversation with Libby.

"Richard, I'm sure that I heard voices in Libby's room," stated Libby's mother.

"She must be talking to her doctor, or one of the nurses," he softly responded

"One of the nurses told me that quite often, just before a patient dies, they get an endorphin rush in their brain, sit up and start blabbing away," Libby's sister Dawn offered. "They'll talk to themselves and have a good conversation even if there's no one there with them."

"Dawn! Now you're talking crazy!" Libby's mother retorted as the family entered the room. "Libby's sick! She's not nuts! Only crazy people talk to themselves."

"Whatever. Take a look at her. She's the same way we left her."

"No she's not," her father responded. "Libby's gone. She's not breathing. She waited for us to leave before she passed," he somberly added. "She didn't want to be embarrassed and pass on in front of us."

"You knew didn't you Richard? That's why you took us out for breakfast at Denny's."

"Yes. Libby and I had a good talk just before she went into surgery yesterday afternoon. That's what she wanted."

"I figured that's what you were up to and that's why I opened the window."

"I don't understand."

"A nurse that lives a couple of houses down from us told me to do it. She works in the ICU unit at Martin Memorial Hospital North and all of the nurses there believe that they have to open the window in a dying patient's room just before they pass on in order to free their spirit. If they don't open the window the spirit gets trapped in the hospital and wanders the halls for Eternity looking for a way out. You wouldn't want that to happen to Libby's spirit would you?"

"Of course not. Then her spirit's free?"

"Of course. Do you see that faint blue light flickering just outside the window?"

"Yes. So what?"

"That's Libby's spirit telling us that she's okay. Her suffering is over and she's in a better place with lots of pretty blue star sapphires and no pain. She'll be fine and someday we'll be together as a family again."

"I'll miss her a lot," chimed in her younger brother Josh as he turned off his video game and tossed it into the metal trash can beside the vanity. "She yelled at me a lot, but I'll still miss her."

"Me too," added her older sister Dawn. "She listened in on my telephone calls and snuck peeks into my diary, but that's okay. I wanted her to go out for the cheerleading squad next year. I'll be graduating and she was a shoo-in for my spot."

"I'm certain that she'll be there," her mother whispered softly as she pulled Dawn close to her right side and gathered Josh into her side with her left arm. "We'll all be there with her someday."

Libby's father stood behind his family and wrapped his burly arms around all of them in a big bear hug. "I'll miss her too, but we all have to go on with our own lives."

"I'll miss seeing her go out on her first date, talking to her about boys, the thrill of her first kiss and going shopping for a prom dress," her mothered whispered.

"Mom, I told her all about boys, she's been making out with the boy across the street for at least six months and she could've worn my old prom dress."

"Dawn, would you be willing to let Libby wear your prom dress at her funeral?"

"Of course mom! That's a great idea. I'll take it to the dry cleaners tomorrow."

"Richard, what about her eyes?"

"What about them? The surgeons took them out yesterday afternoon."

"I can't let her be buried without her beautiful blue eyes. She needs to have them with her."

"I don't know what they did with them, but I'll find out! Let's go so I can start calling the doctors!"

"It's not even six o'clock. The doctors won't be in their offices until nine o'clock."

"I'll leave messages with their answering service! Let's go!"

"What about Libby?" Josh interjected. "What going to happen to her now?"

"Some hospital attendants will come in, remove her body and take her to the funeral home."

"When will we see her again?"

"At her funeral."

"When will that be?"

"I'm not certain, usually it takes three days to get it set up."

"I guess that's okay."

"Richard, let's take the kids home and let them get some sleep," Libby's mother offered.

"Do we have to go to school today," Josh inquired.

"No son," she replied. "You don't have to go to school today."

"Good. I don't like riding in that dumb school bus. The new driver goes too fast. Yesterday she almost hit a truck coming out of the Rivergate Shopping Center. She had to slam on the brakes and a couple of kids flew out of their seats."

"That's a bad traffic area," his father responded. "What time does your school bus usually pass Rivergate Shopping Center?"

"About seven-thirty."

"I'll call the county transportation department and complain. We don't need for a school bus to get into an accident there." The father gently maneuvered his compact family towards the open door. "Let's go home. Libby would be embarrassed if she knew that we were standing around here."

"Libby knows," his wife replied with a smile as she wiped a tear from her cheek. "She knows and she understands. And it's also okay for us because she knows that we'll be okay."

Chapter
17

Fortunately for me none of Libby's family members had to pee during their brief stay in her room after her gentle passing. I waited until the sound of their voices faded into nothingness and I felt that they had entered the elevator. I was surprised that none of the nurses had dashed down to check on Libby because her pulse and heart monitor had certainly triggered an alarm at the nurses' station.

"*Hey Dumbo! Get out of there quick unless you have to pee!*" Emma's shrill voice echoed in my brain cortex. "*Two nurses are on their way down there and they don't need to know that you're hiding out in the bathroom!*"

"What do you want me to do?" I responded out loud. "I can't disappear!"

"*First of all don't talk me in that tone of voice and second don't talk out loud to me. I can hear your thoughts so let's communicate on a telepathic level. Okay?*"

"*Okay,*" I thought. "*What should I do?*"

"*Slip out of there and slide down the hall back to Room 307.*"

"*That's the Little League Baseball player Tommy Hall's room. I've already seen him!*"

"*It's empty. The little boy's been taken away and the room's empty. They have a patient on the way up there from ICU, but I'll stall them in the elevator.*"

"*Okay. I'm on my way,*" I thought.

"*Hold it! You're too late. The nurses are almost there. Stay in the bathroom and keep your mouth shut. If you want to talk to me just think about what you want to say and I'll pick it up. Don't talk out loud or they'll hear you!*"

"*Okay boss.*"

"*I'm not your boss! I'm just a spirit leading the way for you to get your job done!*"

Two nurses, Marilyn and Cathy entered the room.

"The mother swears she heard her daughter talking to someone when they came back from Denny's," Marilyn stated. "She stood outside the room for a couple of minutes and listened to them."

"Marilyn, do you really think there was someone else in here with her?"

"No. The mother is under a lot of pressure and she hallucinated."

"Maybe we should look in the bathroom?"

"Cathy, do you still imagine that monsters live under your bed too?"

"Of course not!"

"Then who do you think was in here with her?"

"I saw a doctor making rounds about eleven o'clock. Maybe it was he?"

"Maybe, but it's really unusual that she would wake up and hold a conversation with anyone. She was really doped up with morphine. We were giving her four milligrams every hour."

"Oh well, it doesn't matter now. Let's get those IV needles out of her arms and get her cleaned up before the funeral home guys get here."

"Cathy, did you see that blue light flashing outside the

window when we came into the room?"

"Yes, it was probably a reflection from a security vehicle's blue light. Some of those dodos like to drive around the parking lot at night with their blue lights on pretending that they're real cops."

"A male ego trip I suppose."

"Roger on the ego trip."

"Cathy, can I tell you something? I don't want you to laugh at me or think that I'm nuts."

"Marilyn, I already know that you're a 'whack' job. That's why I enjoy working with you. Lay it on me. What's on your mind? A man?"

"Naw. I don't need a man for anything. They're too hard to train and housebreaking is out of the question for most of them. Cathy, you might be right about her talking to someone. I heard voices over the patient monitoring intercom link and I think they came from this room."

"What makes you think that they came from this room?"

"I was sitting at the nurses' station playing solitaire on the computer and accidentally flipped down the 'audio monitor' switch for this room with my elbow. I didn't know that I did it at the time, but I kept hearing voices and thought that I was having delusions. I looked over at the control panel and the green light for this room was lit."

"What did you hear? Was it juicy stuff?"

"I thought that I heard the patient talking and I thought she was talking to a nurse, or perhaps a doctor. I only heard her voice. I thought that perhaps she was talking to herself and trying to make peace with her family before she went."

"Marilyn, those audio monitoring systems can be tricky. The microphone is located in that panel beside the patient's head and they are designed to pick up only one side of a conversation in the room. It would be a violation of the Federal Privacy Act if we were able to listen in on conversations between a patient and their family or doctor."

"Oh. So, I'm not nuts and I wasn't having delusions? I really heard her talking."

"I didn't say that. I doubt that she was talking at all. She never woke up after she came back from surgery. The surgeons removed both of her eyes and she was doped up solid. They didn't want her to wake up and feel any pain."

"Cathy, be honest with me. What do you think I heard?"

"I don't know. Do you often hear voices in your head telling you to do things? That's called schizophrenia. Maybe you should see a shrink? They have a good one on staff here."

"Thanks for the vote of confidence, but I don't think so. I know what I heard."

"Marilyn, do you hear voices in your head right now telling you to pull out those IV's and get the patient cleaned up and ready for transport to the funeral parlor?"

"No."

"You'd better because they're on their way."

"Can you wait a minute? I've got to pee really bad."

"Marilyn! You know better than that! Don't ever use a patient's bathroom! You never know what you might catch. You go ahead and take off for the nurses' bathroom. It's at the end of the hall and to your right. I'll finish up here."

"Cathy, are you sure that you can do this all by yourself?"

"Marilyn old girl, I've been an RN for twelve years and I think that I can handle a catheter and three IV ports. Go before you wet your pants!"

"Okay! I'm going. Call me if you need me."

"Sure. I'll call you over the patient audio monitoring link so you can really hear voices."

"Cathy! You should be ashamed of yourself! Now you're making fun of me! That's not fair!"

"Life isn't fair and neither is death if you haven't noticed. Now go before you pee on the floor."

I chuckled as I tossed around in my mind the embarrassment it would have caused Marilyn if she had come into the bathroom and found me sitting on the toilet. Two of us couldn't share the same seat! Emma's unforgiving wrath interrupted my serious thought process.

"*What kind of pervert are you?*" Emma's sharp, obviously irritated voice dug deeply into my brain's cortex. "*What are you doing thinking about a nurse sitting on a toilet and urinating?*"

"Emma!" I muttered under my breath. "What did I do?"

"Shut up! I told you not to talk out loud. That other nurse might hear you and come in the bathroom to check."

"Okay. I hear you."

"No you don't! I'm communicating with you via mental telepathy. Just think what you want to say to me and don't talk out loud. Okay?"

"Okay."

"Stop talking, start thinking when you communicate with me and stop thinking about that nurse peeing and get out of there."

"What about the other nurse?" I thought very hard when I communicated with Emma and it made my brain hurt!

"She's tidying up the room. On second thought stay in there. I want to talk to you about your next patient in Room 309. It's a very sad case."

"Have you already opened the window? If you have then it's a waste of my time."

"There you go with that snotty attitude again! I told you that you're the medical doctor and I'm only an evaluator."

"You evaluate them right out of the window before I get in to see them!"

"I always take your objective evaluation into account before I make my subjective decision."

"It's always going to be your call isn't it?"

"Yep. Now stop your yapping and let me fill you in on the next patient."

"Okay. Go ahead and do your thing. I'm ready to lose another one."

"There you go with that defeatist attitude again! Just listen to what I have to say!"

"I'm all ears."

"Your ears don't have anything to do with it. You hear me telepathically."

"You said that before. Do you mind if I take a pee while you're sending your message?"

"Go right ahead, but don't do it standing up! Sit down on the toilet seat."

"I'm not a female. I pee standing up."

"If you pee standing up the nurse will hear the 'tinkling' when your urine hits the water and she might come in to investigate the noise."

"She might like what she sees."

"Shut up, sit down, pee your brains out and pay attention."

"May I flush the toilet when I'm done peeing?"

"No! *Why don't you just shoot a red flare down the center of the hallway? That way you will be certain to call attention to yourself."*

"I'll try to hold it until the nurse leaves. Tell me about my next patient."

"His name's Jim. He's a Fort Pierce native and he has terminal melanoma that's spread to the major organs of his body and his brain. He's been struggling to stay alive, but it's a lost case."

"So? You'll open the window before I get in to see him and he'll be on his way. Why bother?"

"Listen to me carefully. Jim married a real bimbo twenty-two years ago and two years later she ran away to California with a UPS deliveryman. She took their son with her and Jim hasn't seen him in almost five years. He flew out to Los Angeles for his son's high school graduation and they had dinner together. That's the last time he saw him."

"So?"

"Jim knows that he is in the final stages of his disease and doesn't have much time left. He wants to see his son and make peace with him before he dies."

"Why doesn't he call his son, ask him to fly into West Palm Beach, rent a car and drive up here?"

"It's not that easy. Jim's son enlisted in the Army right after high school graduation and he's serving in a top-secret unit. No one can contact him directly and he's not permitted to contact his family for fear of compromising his unit."

"Where is he now?"

"It's top-secret and I can't tell you."

"I'll bet a buck that you don't know. You're bluffing."

"Yes I do! I'm a spirit and I can find out anything!"

"No you can't. You don't know where he is do you?"

"Yes I do! He's in Iraq."

"Thank you. Why don't you contact his unit commander and explain that his father is dying and wants to see his son? I'm certain that they'll grant him emergency family leave and get him on the first flight out of Baghdad."

"I can't do that."

"Why not? You're a spirit and you can do anything."

"I can't interfere in future events that would change history, besides I'm a spirit and he wouldn't be able to see or hear me!"

"I can hear you and sometimes I can even see you."

"You can hear me because I chose to communicate with you, actually I was ordered to do it, and you can only see me when I want you to see me."

"Then what am I supposed to do?"

"Be cool, talk to Jim and tell him that his son's on the way to see him."

"But that's not true."

"We don't know that for certain. He might be, that is if the nurses got through to his ex-wife, and she was able to contact their son. But there's a big problem there too."

"Great! Why didn't you call it a challenge? Isn't that the politically correct term?"

"Because it's not a challenge. It's a very big problem."

"Oh that's just great! A supervisor once told me that problems are opportunities in work clothes. I never liked him after that. Why is it a very big problem?"

"Jim's ex-wife got married for the third time two days ago and she's off on her honeymoon."

"Does anyone know where she went?"

"When the supervising nurse called her home in Los Angeles she got an answering machine message that said she was on a honeymoon cruise to St. Thomas in the British Virgin Islands and will return in ten days. That will be too late for Jim. She didn't specify what cruise line and besides, even if we could find out, passenger manifests are closely-guarded secrets."

"What do you expect me to do? Did you already open his window?"

"No! He's not quite ready to go. He needs to make peace with

*his son first, or his spirit will never rest. I don't need him
wandering around this place at all hours of the day and night.
It's already crowded."*

"So, I'll ask you again. What do you expect me to do?"

*"Try to help him make peace with himself and to understand
that what happened between him and his wife wasn't his fault."*

"How can I do that? I don't know what happened."

"He'll tell you. He likes to talk."

"What about his son? When will he get here?"

*"I don't know. Just stall for time until I get more information.
I sent 'Spirit Resources' an e-mail and asked for a waiver of the
contact rule in this case. But, with all the red tape and approvals
that are required it might take a few days."*

"Does he have a few days?"

"He has as much time as we choose to give him."

*"What do you mean we? You're the one that kicks them out of
the open window!"*

*"You're part of this too! I count on your recommendation
before I do anything. You know that. Get in there and get going.
He's waiting for you to make your rounds."*

"How does he know I'm coming?"

*"I woke him up a few minutes ago and told him. Go break a
leg."*

*"No thanks. I did that once when I was playing football. I
don't want to do it again."*

*"That's just an expression used in the theater. It means to get
out there and do your best."*

"Okay. I'm going. Where are you going to be if I need you?"

*"I'll be in the Emergency Room and Intensive Care Unit. I
need to clear out a few beds before those kids from the school bus
accident on Port St. Lucie Boulevard start rolling in here about
seven-thirty."*

"Why don't you warn someone, or do something to stop it?"

*"I can't. The bus accident's not going to occur until my shift is
over. Besides if I warned someone it would be a serious violation
of the changing of future events regulation. I'd get a nasty
reprimand letter in my personnel file, be fined at least a dozen
'atta boy' points and most likely be transferred out of here to*

boot. You'd like that wouldn't you?"

"I'd like what?"

"If they shipped me out to Ocala, Yee Haw Junction, or some other remote location."

"No, I wouldn't. I've gotten used to you following me around on rounds the last three years."

"Is that a compliment?"

"No."

"Oh. That's too bad. I have to go now. I'll check on how you're making out with Jim later. Bye."

I shrugged my shoulders, opened the bathroom door just a crack and peeked into the room. It was dark, the door was closed and the bed was stripped of sheets. It was ready for the next client. I flipped on the bathroom light, heard the exhaust fan 'whir' into high gear, flipped the toilet seat up and unzipped my pants. I had to pee really bad and no one was going to stop me.

Chapter
18

Emma left me in a lurch and I had no idea as to what I was going to tell Jim about his condition or his son. I reached for the clipboard standing awkwardly upright in the clear plastic holder mounted beside the door to Room 309. I silently read the generic cover sheet to myself.

"Jim was diagnosed with extreme melanoma two years earlier. He is forty-eight years old, six foot one inch tall and weighs one hundred and fifty-two pounds. He's single and his next of kin is listed as being his son, but there is no address shown for him. Jim executed a Living Will and 'Health Care Surrogate' form upon admission to the hospital three days earlier. His son is listed as the responsible party on both documents."

I tucked the clipboard under my left arm, took a deep breath and entered Room 309. It was game time and I was going to do my best to break a leg. Jim was sitting up in bed and when he saw me come in a wide grin spread across his freckled face. He reminded me of a middle-aged Howdy Doody.

"It's about time that you got here Doc," he quipped in deep voice drenched with a southern twang. " I was wondering if I'd fallen off your radar screen."

"I'm here now Jim," I cautiously replied. "How do you feel?"

"Like a pile of dog crap! I'm dying of cancer. How do you expect I'd feel?"

"Like crap I suppose," I replied because I couldn't think of anything else to say.

"Look at me doc! I'm a living skeleton, my hair's falling out in big clumps because of the damn radiation treatments and chemotherapy and they've got a plastic tube stuck up my pecker so I won't wet the bed."

"I understand."

"Have you been in this position before?"

"No."

"Then how could you know how I feel"

"What I meant to say Jim is that I've seen many patients in the same condition that you are in over the years."

"You do know that I'm dying don't you?"

"We are all in the process of dying from the moment we're born. Mother's Nature's hour glass begins draining out the contents of our life at the exact moment of birth."

"I'm only forty-eight years old! I feel shortchanged! Did somebody else steal some of my sand?"

"I don't think anyone would steal anyone else's sand. God doles out the exact amount of sand that matches our own individual life span. When it runs out your time's up."

"Big deal! I'm not ready for my sand to run out. I still need to see my boy before I check out and he's on the way. He'll be here soon."

"Where's he coming from?"

"He's in the Army. He's assigned to a handpicked special operations unit that's more secret than the DELTA Force."

"Where's he stationed?" I tried my best to play along and pretend that I knew nothing, but I felt that he could see right through my charade.

"He can't say because what he does is top-secret. The last time

I talked to him he was on his way to Bosnia and that was a few years ago. He's not allowed to write letters and can only call us collect from a pay phone when he's in the states."

"Oh. How did you get in touch with him to tell him that you're in the hospital?"

"I didn't. My wife will do it. She knows some influential people in Washington."

"Your wife? Your file indicates that you're not married."

"We got divorced twenty years ago after she ran off to California with a UPS guy. But I still call her my wife."

"Did you speak to her personally?"

"No. One of the nurses called her yesterday and filled her in on the details. My son will make it in time. He knows that I need to talk to him before I go."

"Do you have something special that you want to tell him?"

"I want to tell him that I love him and I'm proud of him. I've never told him that."

"Jim, tell me a little about yourself." I was stalling for time.

"What do you want to know? My life's an open book."

"Where do you grow up? Are you a Florida native?"

"Yes and proud of it! I was born in Fort Pierce and my daddy was one of the original treasure hunters in this area. He was digging up gold coins on the beach before anyone else suspected that there was treasure strewn all along the beach between Stuart and Sebastian."

"Do you have any brothers or sisters?"

"No. I'm an only child. My father got hurt in a diving accident and he couldn't father any more children. He figures that's why my momma left him. She wanted more kids."

"*Come on Emma*," I thought to myself. "*I'm stalling for time and I'm starting to sound stupid!*"

"Did you say something doctor?"

"No. Maybe I was thinking out loud. Where did you go to school?"

"I graduated from Fort Pierce Central and attended the University of Miami on a football scholarship until I got hurt and they dropped me like a hot potato."

"What happened?"

"I dropped out of college and became a charterboat captain."

"No, what I meant was how did you get hurt playing football?"

"I didn't get hurt playing ball. I got drunk during a spring break party, jumped out of a third floor hotel window into the swimming pool and broke both of my legs. It wasn't pretty."

"So, you became a charterboat captain? Tell me about that?"

"*Come on Emma!*" I thought with all the strength my brain's cortex could muster. There was no response.

"There isn't much to tell. I studied hard, drove to Miami, took the Coast Guard's Six Pak exam and passed it on the first try. They typed up my license on the spot and I filed for my fifth license renewal last month."

"How long is a Coast Guard license good for?"

"Five years."

"You said something about a Six Pak license. What does that mean?"

"That means I can only carry six paying passengers on my boat."

"*Come on Emma! Talk to me,*" my brain screamed. "*I'm dying here.*" There was no response.

"Tell me what have the doctors told you about your illness?"

"I've got a bad case of melanoma and the cancer has spread to my liver, pancreas, lungs and spine. They haven't told me if it's reached my brain. They did a CT Scan of my head yesterday afternoon. They know if it's in my brain, but they haven't told me. That's what scares me the most."

"What scares you the most?"

"If the cancer's in my brain. I don't want to go crazy and start having fits."

"I don't think there's much chance of that happening. We have many types of medications to control it."

"What can you control? The cancer?"

"No, the convulsions if the cancer has invaded your brain," I offered.

"*Crap!*" I thought. "*Now I've really put my foot in my mouth.*"

"Jim, when did you find out that you had melanoma?"

"As you can see by what's left of my red hair and freckles I was a fair-skinned kid. I got a lot of bad sunburns when I was a teenager and it came back to haunt me. We thought it was fun to get a sunburn and we laughed about it."

"You are correct. The recent research indicates that many people who contract melanoma got sunburned many times when they were younger. There wasn't any such thing as sunscreen back then."

"It's my fault. When I was running a charterboat I knew that I should use sunscreen when I went out, but I didn't. My macho mindset wouldn't allow it and I didn't want to be called a *wuss* by the other guys."

"Did you ever hear that expression that starts out Sticks and stones can break my bones?"

"Yeah and names can never hurt me. It's too late for that now."

"Let's get back to my original question? When did you learn that you had contracted melanoma?"

"I was swimming in the condo's pool one day and having a good time teasing the broads and one of them got a little wild and took a swipe at me with her claws. She missed my face but she scratched the top off of a red mark on my chest while in the swimming pool. The top came off, it didn't heal up and a few days later it turned black with scalloped edges. I went to a dermatologist out on East Ocean Boulevard and he took a sample for testing. That hurt like hell!"

"Biopsies can sting a little."

"Sting my ass! It hurt like hell and I bled like a stuck pig for two days."

"That's normal. Melanomas require a lot of nourishment and they draw neighboring blood vessels into their core. What treatment did the dermatologist recommend?"

"The first thing he did was get me in the operating room and he took a chunk of meat out of my chest the size of a golf ball! He told me that he got all of it and put me on radiation and chemo."

"How did you take to the chemo?" I was getting desperate. "*Emma! Where are you?*" My mind screamed. "*Get up here and help me out!*" There was no response.

"I got sick as a dog and most of my hair fell out. It wasn't fun."

"What did he do for follow up treatments?"

"He made me come to his office once a month for a thorough going over. He always checked the lymph nodes in my neck and under my arms."

"*That's usually the first place a malignant melanoma shows up after radical surgery,*" I thought to myself. "*Once the cancer enters the lymph system it can travel throughout the body unabated.*"

"Doc! Are you still with me?"

"Oops. I must have dozed off. My shift's almost over and I'm tuckered out. I apologize. What we were talking about?"

"You asked me what type of follow up treatments the dermatologist did. I told you that he always poked around the lymph nodes in my neck and under my arms."

"Did he tell you why?"

"He said something about the cancer cells using the lymph system to travel through the body."

"That's correct. Did he find any signs of the melanoma in your lymph nodes?"

"Yes."

"What action did he take?"

"He sent me back into surgery and stripped the lymph nodes out of my neck and from under my arms. It hurt like hell."

"Did they do a biopsy to determine if the melanoma had spread and if so how far it had traveled?"

"He said that my lymph nodes and lymph glands were full of cancer. He sent portions of them to some experimental lab in California and some to a lab in France. They have chemicals in France that kill melanoma, but the FDA won't allow the French to export into the United States."

"That's to protect patients like you from coming in contact with non-proven drugs."

"I thought it was to protect the American drug manufacturers from competition."

"That could be part of it."

"What happened to the samples? Did the California

experimental lab find a drug that would kill your cancer cells?"

"No! A month later some bimbo called my doctor and told him that a new lab technician out there got my lymph nodes mixed up with someone else's and they had to be destroyed because they didn't know which samples were mine and which ones were the other guy's."

"What did your doctor do then?"

"Not a hell of a lot! I didn't have any lymph nodes left in my neck, or under my arms. Plus, the testing was expected to take at least two months and by then it would be too late for me."

"What did you do?"

"I flew out to Los Angeles and tried alternative cancer therapy. I took coffee enemas, had peach pits shoved up my butt and rolled around in some green crap that smelled like swamp gunk."

"What was the result? Did your cancer go into remission?"

"I dropped ten thousand bucks out there and had nothing to show for it except a sore butt hole and armpits that smelled like a swamp. It didn't bother the cancer. I think it liked the peach pits."

"Did you come back here afterwards for a more traditional cancer treatment?"

"No. I jumped a plane to Mexico City, got a penthouse suite in the Marriott and ordered in six hookers, three cases of Tequila and a big box of limes. I lost two weeks and another ten grand in Mexico City. But Doc, do you want to know what the worst thing was about it?"

"Sure. Let me guess. You got married in Mexico City and brought back one of the hookers?"

"No. I don't think so. If she's here I haven't seen her around the condo. The worst thing is that I don't remember a damn thing about it. But I musta' have had a good time."

"How could you tell if you didn't remember anything?"

"The skin was wore clean off my knees and my pecker was sore for a week."

"Did you experience a burning sensation when you urinated?"

"No! I didn't have the clap! I just about wore the damn thing out."

"Do your parents still live in Fort Pierce?"

"No. They were killed in a multi-car crash out on I-95 two years ago. They were on the way to Stuart to attend my son's going away party before he shipped out overseas."

"I'm sorry."

"That's okay. I'm kinda' all alone doc, but my son will be here tomorrow, or the next day."

"Jim, are there any things that you regret doing, or not doing?"

"No. I did pretty much everything I wanted to do. Except I didn't spend much time with my son because my wife took him out to California."

"Didn't you go out to see him?"

"No! She told him that I beat her when we were married and that's why she ran away with the UPS guy. She said that he didn't want to see me."

"Did you beat your wife?"

"Of course not! That's why it's important that I see my son and make things right between him and me before I check out. He has to know the truth about what happened."

"*Emma! Where are you*," I screamed through the cortex of my brain. I felt the blood drain out of my brain and I felt light-headed. There was no response. She knew that she dealt me a card off the bottom of the deck. There was no chance of me winning this round and she knew it.

"Doc, are you okay?" Jim asked. "Did you faint?"

"No, I'm okay," I softly responded. "I just felt a little light-headed for a minute. I haven't had anything to eat since about six o'clock last night. I need a sugar fix."

"There's a cute Phillipino nurse up there that can give you a little sugar if she has any to spare."

"Let's not go there. Jim, I just felt a draft on the back of my neck. Did you feel it?"

"It's not a draft. Some lady slipped in while you were talking and opened the window."

"*Emma! Why did you do this to me again?*"

Chapter
19

I slipped out of Jim's room into the empty hallway and leaned against the wall for support. I felt hyperglycemic and needed a sugar fix! The clock on the wall across from the nurses' station read 6:17 and the hospital cafeteria had been open for seventeen minutes. *"Maybe I can sneak down there and get a hot cup of coffee with two sugars before I go in to interview the patient in Room 310,"* I thought. Thinking was my first mistake!

"You don't have time for a cup of coffee!" Emma's shrill voice echoed in my brain. *"You still have one more patient to see before you can clock out!"*

"Emma! Why don't you go about your own business and leave me alone?" I muttered out loud. "Haven't you done enough damage for tonight?"

"What do you mean damage? I'm only doing my job. Maybe you think you could do it better?"

"I don't want your job, but I know that I could do it better."

"You sound just like an egotistical man! Exactly what would you do differently?"

"I wouldn't spend so much time looking for patients that I could wipe out. You don't give them a chance. Just when they seem to be coming around you pop in, open the window and throw them out!"

"Maybe, just maybe, you don't understand what my job responsibilities are."

"I think I do. You told me."

"Okay! What are they and who do I answer too if I screw up?"

"You are a self-appointed triage department. You interview and evaluate patients before you give them their walking papers, rip out their soul and drive it out of the window."

"I don't rip out their soul! I provide their spirit with guidance so they aren't afraid of dying. Soul capture and rejection come under another department. I work for the Spirit Resources Department."

"What do you call it when you push a nine year old boy who wants to be a professional baseball player, a nine year old girl with brain cancer and a thirteen year old blind girl out of the window?"

"I don't push them out of the window! I provide their spirit with a path so it doesn't get locked in the hospital for Eternity like mine! You'll understand what I'm doing very soon."

"I don't think its right! People should be allowed to pass on their own terms."

"Look here doctor! The Emergency Room is backed up and seven critical patients are on gurneys in the hall because they can't get them into the Intensive Care Unit because no one's checked out for at least an hour. And patients can't move up here from the ICU until I make some bed space for them! It's a never-ending, thankless circle. I make a lot of difficult decisions every night and I'm beat at the end of my shift."

"Let's have a poor Emma cheer. Poor Emma!"

"You dumb ass doctors just can't understand that you can't save every patient? There's not enough beds for all of them. Some of them have to go to make room for the others that are right behind them."

"That's a poor way to look at it."

"Then you tell me what's going to happen if I don't clean out the third floor tonight and make room for ten patients to move up here from ICU? That school bus is going to hit that truck at seven twenty-seven no matter what you or I do. The ER is going to need some open beds and so is the ICU. This is no different from working at a dog pound. Every dog, cat, puppy and kitten is cute and cuddly, but they have to move out some inventory every day to make room for the new ones. They know that they can't save everyone and neither can you. Face it doc! It's life!"

"I still don't like it Emma. I was trained to save lives."

"You were also trained to relieve physical suffering."

"But I'm not able to give them any medication to help them and I feel useless!"

"You are doing much more than what medication can accomplish. You're finally talking to patients, understanding them and finding out what makes them tick. You're helping them find mental peace with themselves. That's better medicine than anything that pours out of a bottle or comes in a tablet."

"But I don't want all of them to die."

"Death is a natural part of life. You know that."

"But some of them could go on for a few more days."

"At what quality of life? When the sand's run out of the hourglass it's time for them to go."

"Emma, I can see that we are at opposite ends of a philosophical argument and we could go on all night and neither of us would ever convince the other. What's with the next patient?"

"Aren't you jumping the gun?"

"What do you mean? It's almost six-thirty and I still have to see one more patient."

"Big deal! So do I. Don't you want to know about Jim and why he went so easily?"

"I'm not very pleased with you. You sandbagged me."

"What do you mean I sandbagged you?"

"You let me string him along that his son was coming to see him and then you booted him out of the window. He didn't get to see his son. That's all he wanted before he died."

"*Yes he did.*"

"What? His son didn't make it to the hospital in time."

"*Jim's son is with him right now.*"

"How can that be? I didn't see anyone come in."

"*You are correct morphine breath. No one came in and no one left the room.*"

"Then you have to explain it to me. I must be dense as a log."

"*You are. Do you remember when you were screaming and hollering for me to come back here and bail you out?*"

"I wasn't screaming and I wasn't hollering. I was thinking. You told me that you communicate with me telepathically."

"*To me it was screaming. I could hear you just fine, but I couldn't answer you.*"

"Why not?"

"*I was on special assignment for about a half hour.*"

"Where?"

"*Overseas.*"

"What? I thought that I heard you say that you were on assignment overseas?"

"*That's correct. They had an emergency and needed an experienced triage spirit.*"

"Now this is really getting ridiculous!"

"*Is it? You're the one standing out here in the hall talking to yourself. The nurses are looking at you and trying to decide if they should call someone to take you away. Try thinking and stop talking.*"

"*Okay,*" I thought as I attempted to make it appear to the staring nurses that I was dictating notes into the right sleeve of my lab coat. "*Is this better?*" I thought as I wrinkled my brow. This thinking business is hard work!

"*Much better. Now do you want to know where I was and why I was there?*"

"I suppose that I don't have much choice because you going to tell me anyway," I thought.

"*I don't have to tell you anything, but a few minutes ago you were ragging on me about helping Jim's spirit escape this damnable hospital. It had to be done at exactly that time. No sooner. No later.*"

"Why?"

"I was in Iraq helping out a triage unit. There was a Rocket Propelled Grenade attack on an Army unit that was operating undercover in plain clothes inside the Sunni Triangle. Six guys were killed outright and six others were severely wounded by shrapnel. I helped the Baghdad unit make the necessary decisions in order to keep the ER cleared out."

"Why did you have to be there? Doesn't Spirit Resources have a big enough budget to keep those units fully staffed with experienced triage spirits?"

"Jim's son was one of those six badly wounded soldiers. He didn't make it. I had to coordinate his spirit release with Jim's so that they could rendezvous. They're together now."

"What about Jim's wife?"

"What about her?"

"Did she try to contact Jim's son and let him know that Jim was dying?"

"Of course not. She's on her third honeymoon on a cruise ship somewhere in the Caribbean. Do you have yourself together enough so that you can see your last patient for this shift?"

"I suppose so. Who is it? What's the patient's name?"

"Is the name important? If I told you who it was would you recognize the name?"

"I suppose not."

"You supposed correctly and you wouldn't. The patient in Room 310 is an eighty-year old female with congestive heart failure, diabetes, a total cholesterol count that normally runs about four hundred, and double bronchial pneumonia. She was on a respirator in ICU for two days and ordered the nurses to remove it on Friday afternoon. She's refused all of her normal medications and has been here since Friday."

"What are her chances?"

"Zero to none. Her oxygen level was ninety-two at six o'clock and dropping fast."

"What's her name?"

"Why is her name so important to you?"

"I'd like to be able to call her by name when I go in to see her."

"Her name is Betty."

"Betty what?'

"Betty McElroy. Are you happy now?"

"McElroy? Where have I heard that last name before?"

"Her son's an author. He's written several novels featuring the Treasure Coast as a locale."

"Why kind of novels?"

"Mysteries."

"Maybe he'll write a book about us?"

"I doubt it. We're no mystery."

"Doctor! Are you okay?" Inquired a soft female voice off my right shoulder. "You appear to be talking to someone, but there's no one here."

Startled by the voice I turned slightly to the left, so that she couldn't see my face, and attempted an intelligent response. "I'm fine and thank you for asking. I'm dictating the last patient's notes into a new digital tape recorder. The remote, voice-activated microphone is mounted in the sleeve of my lab coat. Would you like to try it?" I lifted my right arm in her direction.

"No thanks. But you were talking into your left sleeve."

"I know. I was just joking with you. It's late and I need some sleep. What can you tell me about the patient in Room 310?"

"I heard you dictating and you already know that her name is McElroy. How did you know that without reading her chart? It's still hanging on the door."

"A little voice in my head told me. I'm telepathic."

"Oh. She's an eighty year-old female suffering from congestive heart failure and double bronchial pneumonia. She refused all of her meds on Friday and we have her on four milligrams of morphine every three hours for pain and comfort. She won't last much longer."

"Doesn't she also suffer from diabetes?"

"Yes! You must have read her chart before I came up to you."

"You caught me!" I kept my head turned away from her in order avoid accidental eye contact. "I had already scanned the summary sheet, placed her chart back into the holder and was dictating notes into my sleeve when you came up and spoke to me."

"Oh. Doctor, is there a particular reason why you turned away when I spoke to you? Do I have bad breath or something? You can tell me. I'm a big girl and I can take rejection."

"No. Your breath is fine. The zipper on my pants broke. I can't seem to get it to zip back up and I'm a little embarrassed."

"I understand. It happens to my husband all the time. Would you like me to help you? I'm very good with stuck zippers."

"I'll bet you are, but no thanks. This is embarrassing enough. Please don't tell the other nurses about it."

"I won't. Would you like me to accompany you when you visit the next patient?"

"No thank you. I prefer to be alone when I meet with my patients. I've found over the years that they open up better to me if I'm alone."

"Okay. Have it your way," the nurse snottily quipped as she turned and headed towards the nurses' station. I kept my head turned away from her just in case she decided to look backwards.

"Well! You almost got your butt in trouble that time didn't you? That broad thinks that you're nuts because she saw you talking to yourself and when you told her that your zipper was broken she came into immediate heat!"

"Emma! Where are you?"

"Where I always am. Inside your head I don't want to risk having her see me too."

"What do you want now? Are you preparing me for another one of your surprises?"

"No surprises. I promise. I feel very sorry for the patient in Room 310 and I want you to be very nice to her. She won't be here for very much longer."

"I suppose that you have to move her out to make room for someone from the ICU?"

"No. The ICU bed situation is under control and so is the ER's. That is until that busload of injured kids comes in at seven thirty-eight. My shift's over at seven and then it'll be somebody else's problem."

"Why do you feel sorry for her?"

"Physically she's very sick, but mentally she's not quite ready to go. She still has some things that she wants to do, but her

time's up. The hourglass is almost empty and she has to go today."

"Can't you give her some more time? A day or two perhaps?"

"That's out of my control. Her body's shot and it just can't go any longer. Her lungs are filling up with congestion and her heart is worn out. Will you spend some extra time with her and help her understand that she has to go?"

"I'm a medical doctor not a psychiatrist! I was trained to dispense medications to make people well, not to be their camp counselor."

"You are making this very hard on me doctor. You don't have a choice! Get in there and make that poor woman feel better and while you're at it make her understand that she has to stop fighting it. You have an excellent bedside manner. Convince her to close her eyes and go to sleep. I'll be waiting for her outside her window."

"Why don't you tell her? Why should it be my job?"

"Because Chapter four, section twelve point six of the Spirit Handbook specifically states that it is not the function of a spirit guide to convince a patient to die, but to simply lead them through the window and guide them to Eternity."

"But you've been wiping out patients all night long in order to free up beds!"

"That's true I suppose, but I only pointed the way and led them to where they were going. I didn't have to convince any of them to pass over. Only a medical doctor is authorized to urge a patient to let go based on objective medical facts and no hope for recovery. You of all people should know that!"

"I guess I did but I was in denial. What do you want me to tell her?"

"If you feel that's it's appropriate, after you've made your objective medical analysis, for her to give up the ghost and that's only a figure of speech, then tell her that it's okay to go."

"I've told relatives of my patients to do that, but I've never done it myself."

"Why don't you try it? You might like it."

"Okay. You win. I'll give it a shot."

"Good! Now stop talking into your sleeve! Six nurses at the

end of the hall are staring at you and I'm out of here!"

"Where are you going? Don't leave me now!"

"*Now isn't that a big turn around. The big man wants me to hang around and wipe his nose. My shift is just about over. I'll be here if you need me. Bye.*"

"Emma! Don't leave me!" I pleaded into my left sleeve, but I knew that she was gone.

I reached down to my crotch, pretended to zip up my fly, turned and reached for the patient's chart that was tucked into the clear plastic holder mounted on the wall.

The summary sheet didn't tell me anything that I didn't already know. This was one sick lady! I coughed twice to clear my throat and headed for the open door of Room 310. It's 6:27 A.M. I still have a half hour before my shift is over.

Chapter
20

I wasn't ready to face the finality of another life. I needed time to compose myself and get my act together. I leaned back against the wall, closed my eyes and tried to rationalize the events of the past few hours. I needed sleep desperately and felt that I was becoming slightly delusional. However, I was still able to think and hold a semi-intelligent one-sided conversation with myself.

"*Life is indeed strange,*" I mused. "*Our birth is actually the beginning of the end of our life cycle. At the exact moment of our birth Mother Nature's hourglass of time is flipped over and our individual grains of fine white sand begin their trek downward and through the narrow opening at the neck into the empty chasm below. At first look it appears that the large amount of silicon granules in the top half of the hourglass will take an Eternity to filter through the narrow opening and be gone. But it passes through much too quickly and life, as we mortals know it, comes to an end.*"

I smiled, adjusted my tired shoulders for a slightly better position against the wall and continued my philosophy soliloquy.

"A baby is born, nursed, weaned, potty-trained, nursed through a multitude of normal childhood illnesses, nurtured through primary school, tolerated while in middle school and undergoing the rigors of adolescence. At this point in time it seems impossible that they will finally reach high school, the dangerous dating and driving years, and at last graduate. Then they can be coaxed to finally move out of the house! But, then in the middle age years, one looks back at massive photo albums filled with repetitious photographs of the same people and wonders where did time go?"

I slightly shifted my position against the wall and continued to muse. *"Children start their lives in soiled diapers and in turn will eventually help their own parents go out in soiled diapers! What a paradox!"* I was stalling for time because I didn't want to see the last patient! I read clearly between the lines and Emma was waiting to pounce on her last victim!

My own life was filled with ups and downs; pluses and minuses, fears and joys intermixed with long periods of no meaning. Medical school was a snap, but I don't know where the time went. I spent my residency in limbo and after twenty-two years of roaming these same halls from eleven to seven every night here I still am doing the same thing. Making night rounds isn't a job to me and I could do it for Eternity.

I only have one remaining patient to see before I can clock out and enjoy a hot cup of coffee in the hospital cafeteria. Then it's off to bed for a few hours of sleep, a microwaved snack for dinner, a short nap and the short ride back to the hospital for night rounds at eleven o'clock. I was never married so I don't have to worry about what my wife thinks about my routine and late hours. I have gotten used to the normal cycle of birth to death and recognize that each is the beginning of the other.

"Some believe that the release of a spirit from a physical body allows that spirit to enter the body of a newborn immediately upon exiting the birth canal," I mused as my mind continued drifted further and further into deep philosophical discourse. *"I'm not certain about that in my own mind because I have met many*

spirits over the years, including my old friend Emma, who vacated their physical body but remained where they were physically when they passed. I like the term 'passed' because it does not indicate death, but simply passing from a short-termed dimension into Eternity, a dimension which we as humans do not understand. I have seen dying patients sit straight up in bed and claim to be seeing angels coming to get them and then settling back into their pillow with a sigh of contentment and passing." I was on a roll! Plato and Socrates would be proud of me.

"Where do spirits go and why don't they come back to tell us that they are doing well?" I wondered as I wiggled my shoulders against the wall and continued my musing. *"Are they really there? Or are they simply an irrational electrical synapse of brain neurons gone wild that allows us to see things that are actually not there? The nurses feel Emma's presence, but they can't see her. Why not? Emma told me that she decides who can see her. She has a reason for allowing me to see her and it concerns me because patients in their last stage of life are able to see and talk to her. Am I in the last stage of my life? Is Emma calling me out next?"* Reality snuck in with an unexpected big bang!

"You can bet your sweet ass that I'm calling you out! Wake up and get your butt into Room 310 pronto!" Emma's shrill voice echoed in my brain's inner cortex. *"The patient needs to see you and she's running out of time! It's six thirty-two and she can't hold on for much longer."*

Once again I'd been 'zapped' by a restless spirit! That makes my point.

"By the way, Plato and Socrates wanted me to tell you that your thoughts are crap!"

I shook my head, snapped my eyes open and scanned the hallway through a fuzzy haze. The nurses were busy briefing the dayshift staff on the status of their patients and changes that occurred overnight. There were a lot of new patients on the floor thanks to Emma's dedication to keeping the patient flow moving from the ER through the ICU and up to the third floor. She'd been a busy girl!

"You bet I've been busy. I've only got one more patient to go

before shift change at seven o'clock and I'm not going to tell you again! Get into Room 310 now!"

"Yes Ma'am," I stuttered and then thought to myself. *"Why is she telling me what to do? I'm the doctor on this floor."*

"I'm the Spirit Chaser and you're not going to keep me from meeting my quota! I'm number one on the leader board and I intend to stay there!"

It was then that I finally realized that my presence wasn't really needed to evaluate anyone. I was there as 'window dressing' to facilitate Emma in her role. I shook my head and headed for Room 310 and the certainly of witnessing Death once again. I didn't like it one bit, but I had no choice.

I slipped as silently into the room as I could. The patient's son was fast asleep in a chair next to his mother's bedside, snoring like an Iowa hog, and holding his mother's left hand in his own. She stirred, opened her eyes and sat up when I approached her bedside.

"Shush!" Betty ordered as she sat up in bed. "He's been here with me for the past five nights and he's very tired. He doesn't realize that it's hard for me to go when he's here."

"Why don't you tell him to leave?"

"I can't do that to him. He's my son and he wants to be with me when I pass."

"So Betty, what are you going to do?"

"I made my peace with him last night and I'm ready to go. He was trying to write something on his laptop computer about ten o'clock, but I told him that the light from the screen bothered my eyes and I asked him to turn it off."

"Did he?"

"Yes."

"Did the light from his laptop really bother you?"

"Of course not! I wanted him to relax and go to sleep so he wouldn't see me pass. I want to be with his father so bad. I hurt all over."

"Please tell me about yourself."

"Do I have time?"

"You have all the time you need."

"Where should I start?"

"At the beginning."

"Where should I stop?"

"Right here and right now. It's almost over and only you can deicide when it's time."

"Are you a real doctor?"

"Yes, I'm a real doctor. I've been making night rounds in this hospital for twenty-two years."

"I was born October 5, 1924 in Corry, Pennsylvania."

"Did you have a good childhood?"

"It was okay I guess. I was the youngest of seven children. I had four older brothers and two older sisters. But I never met my grandparents."

"Did your parents ever tell you why?"

"No. But my son found out when he checked my family history."

"What did he find out?"

"Both of my parents were half Indian. My father was the son of a German immigrant and an *Abenaki* Indian girl from Fairfax, Vermont. My mother's family comes from Buell's Corners, Pennsylvania which is home for a tribe of Seneca Indians descended from Chief Cornplanter. Her father was a full-blooded Seneca."

"Wasn't Cornplanter the Seneca Indian chief that negotiated with George Washington for the sale of the portion of the Seneca Indian nation that included the Port of Erie."

"Yes. My parents were considered to be half-breeds and in those days the whites didn't associate themselves with Indians. That's why my parents never took me to see my indian grandparents, but I was satisfied to finally find out who they were."

"It won't be long before you'll meet them for the first time, plus your parents, brothers and sisters are all waiting for you on the other side when you pass."

"When am I going?"

"It won't be long now. Has Emma been in to visit with you"

"No! Who's Emma?"

"You'll know her when you see her. She's your spirit guide to the other side. Just follow her when she points the way for you."

"You're doing pretty good Doc, keep it up," Emma's voice drifted through my brain causing me to lose my chain of thought. *"I need a little more time to make arrangements. She's a complicated case."*

"Doctor, are you okay?" Betty asked.

I regained my composure, shook the cobwebs out of my head and responded. "I'm fine. I must have mentally drifted off. I apologize. It's been a very long night for me."

"I understand. It's been a little hectic for me too."

"Betty, why did you come down with bronchial pneumonia? It's treatable in the early stages."

"My own bullheadedness and stupidity. I never wanted to bother anyone when I was sick."

"What do you mean?"

"I didn't want to bother my son and I didn't always tell him what was wrong with me. He always told me that someday I'd come down with a cold and let it go too far. I finally did it!"

"Please explain."

"A couple of weeks ago I came down with a head cold and I tried to treat it myself. But, it turned into bronchitis. I called my doctor and he prescribed an antibiotic for me. However, it got worse and I was hospitalized with what I thought was simple bronchitis. It was actually bronchial pneumonia. I spent eight days in the hospital and was released after my lungs were clear. My son took me home on Sunday, picked up my new medication and did my grocery shopping at Publix. I was feeling pretty good on Sunday."

"If you were given a clean bill of health on Sunday why did you wind up back here again?"

"Do you want the short or long version?"

"The short one. I don't have much time. It's six thirty-eight and I get off at seven o'clock."

"This is Tuesday morning isn't it?"

"Yes."

"The Visiting Nurse came to see me last Monday morning and I was fine. My son and his wife stopped by to see me after they closed their office and brought me my scandal sheets."

"What do you mean by scandal sheet?"

"*The National Inquirer* and *The Globe*. Women understand. We need to know what's going on."

"Okay, so you were feeling good on Monday. What happened on Tuesday?"

"Just hang on! I'm not finished with Monday. The physical therapist stopped by the house at ten-thirty to give me some exercises to do and about one-thirty a health care aide came and gave me a sponge bath. After she left I fixed myself a bowl of home-made soup for lunch."

""How could make home-made soup in your condition?"

"I made it a few weeks earlier when I was still feeling good and froze it in individual packets."

"When were you admitted back into the hospital with pneumonia?"

"On Wednesday. You seem real antsy. Do you want me to tell you my story or not?"

"*She can't go until she gets this off her chest,*" Emma interjected. "*Don't pressure her to hurry. She has all of Eternity ahead of her.*"

"I don't have all day!" I blurted out loud. A major error!

"What did you say doctor?" Betty asked as she sat straight up in bed. "I thought that you wanted to hear my story?"

"*Now you've really put your big foot in your mouth,*" Emma chided. "It *looks like someone is going to put in a little overtime today and I'm going to enjoy watching you get out of this one.*"

"I certainly do," I feebly responded. "I apologize. I'm very tired and my mind wandered."

"You have a lousy bedside manner. I'm going to request another doctor."

"Please don't do that," I pleaded as I took her hand in mine. "I've got a lot of things on my mind."

"Okay. I'll give you one more shot. If my son knew what you said to me he'd wake up and kick your ass."

"I wouldn't want that! He's too big. Please continue."

"Okay. I left off when I fixed my homemade soup on Tuesday afternoon. I took my medication, went back to bed and dozed off. When I woke up I was feeling really lousy."

"Then what?"

"My son called to check on me at nine o'clock that night. He called me every morning and every night at nine o'clock since his father passed away in nineteen ninety-seven. He never missed calling me even when he was out of town. He travels a lot on business."

"So I hear. What did you tell him Tuesday night?"

"I told him that I wasn't feeling very hot."

"Did he suggest calling your doctor, or taking you to the Emergency Room?"

"Yes, he did and I told him to wait and see how I was doing on Wednesday morning."

"Did he call you Wednesday morning?"

"Of course. He called at exactly nine o'clock?"

"And?"

"I couldn't reach the telephone to answer it."

"Why not? Where was the telephone located?"

"It was right on my bed. My husband and I had twin beds and my son built a flat platform for the portable telephone unit to sit on right next to me. It was easy for me to reach it."

"Why didn't you?"

"I couldn't. I had a stroke earlier that morning when I got back into bed from using the bathroom. When the phone rang I was having a grand mal seizure. My arms and legs were flailing all over the place and I couldn't control them."

"Wow! Then what happened?"

"The telephone stopped ringing and I panicked. But I knew that he'd call back."

"Did he?"

"Yes! Exactly five minutes later the telephone rang again."

"What did you do?"

"I rolled over on my left side and knocked the telephone off its holder. I couldn't talk, but I grunted out a few sounds. I sounded like a wild hog rooting in a palmetto berry patch."

"Then what?"

"I heard my son say that he understood and that he was on the way. He had to drive through heavy traffic all the way from downtown Stuart to Port St. Lucie Boulevard and my street, but he made it in twelve minutes flat!"

"Did he stop for red lights?"

"No! But he wasn't going to stop for any cop. He was on the way to check on me."

"What happened when he got to your house? Had you recovered from the grand mal seizure?"

"No! I was flopping uncontrollably all over the bed like a chicken with its head cut off. I couldn't talk and it scared the hell out of him. He called '911' from the kitchen phone, came into my bedroom and held my hand until the paramedics got there."

"What did they say?"

"They asked him if I'd had a stroke before and he told them yes. They loaded me onto a gurney, rolled me out of the house, slid me into the ambulance and took off for the hospital."

"Did your son go with you?"

"They wouldn't allow him in the ambulance, but he followed behind them in his car about two feet off their bumper."

"He's lucky that he didn't have an accident."

"It wasn't luck. I was riding with him."

"How could you be riding with him? You were in the ambulance!"

"My body was in the ambulance. My spirit was with him."

"Had you already passed? Did you know?"

"Yes and yes. When the paramedics got to the house I was in the final stages of death and they knew it. My body temperature had already dropped to ninety-three degrees, but they brought me back on the ride to the hospital. Now I wish they had left well enough alone."

"Why do you say that?"

"Because I never wanted my family to see me like this. It would have been much better if they could have remembered me the way I was when I left the hospital on Sunday."

"Betty, that was an excellent story. However, it's six forty-two and I must go," I mumbled as I stood up to leave. "I have to turn in my reports before the day shift comes on at seven o'clock."

"I'm not finished with my story!"

"*You'd better sit back down and hear her out,*" Emma screeched in my head. "*If her son wakes up and she tells him how you've been behaving he'll kick your skinny ass.*"

"Yes ma'am," I mumbled as I sat back down in the chair. "I apologize. I didn't realize that there is more to your story. My reports can certainly wait a little longer."

"*That's better big guy,*" Emma cooed. "*You don't know when you might see her again.*"

"Betty, please continue," I stammered.

"Good. Certainly you realize that I can't pass until I clear things up."

"I do. What happened after the paramedics got you to the Emergency Room?"

"Well, as I mentioned earlier, I had already passed and was very content with myself. But, those damn doctors in the ER did their thing and brought me back! But, I shouldn't be mad at them. It's their job to save lives."

"Did you have a Living Will requesting that no extraordinary measures be taken?"

"Yes. My son had it with him."

"Why didn't he tell the doctors to allow you to pass?"

"No one came out into the waiting room to ask him and they didn't allow him in the ER to see me until almost twelve-thirty. By that time they'd stuffed a respirator down by throat, sucked my lungs clear of blood and fluid and had gotten my body temperature up to ninety-five degrees."

"He could have told the doctors to let you go."

"One of the ER doctors mentioned it to him, but my son told him that if there was any possibility of bringing me around for them to give me a chance. He meant well because he loves me, but in retrospect I wish that he'd told them to let me go. Right now he's sleeping and I'm ready to go."

"Now? Right now?" I looked at my watch. It read 6:46. I could taste that hot coffee. "What can I do to help you?"

"*Hold it morphine breath!*" Emma barked. "*Do you see me anywhere?*"

"*No,*" I thought. I knew better than to open my mouth. "*But she's ready to go.*"

"*It's not your decision. It's hers and she has more to say before she goes.*"

"*But it's almost time for me to get off,*" I whined in my

thoughts and I made it a good whine.

"It's almost time for me to get off too, but I have all of Eternity if that's what it takes. Give her a few more minutes. Please. Do it for me," Emma was actually asking not demanding.

"Okay Emma," I thought. *"I'll do it for you, but you owe me one."*

"Yeah right. Whatever you say. I owe you one. One of what I don't know."

"Doctor, can you give me an injection of something to get this over with?" Betty asked.

I snapped back to reality. "No. I can't. Is there anything else that you want to tell me?"

"There isn't much to tell except that they shipped me over to the ICU about four o'clock Wednesday afternoon."

"How did you do over there?"

"Not very well. The doctors and nurses were fine, but I knew that my time was up."

"What made you think that?"

"I couldn't talk because of the respirator and tubes down my throat and up my nose. I communicated by pointing at letters on a board with my finger. On Thursday afternoon I used the letter board to ask my son if I had died."

"What did he say?"

"He said 'no' and he lied."

"How did you know that he lied to you?"

"I read it in his face. He never was a good liar. Besides I had already gone over to the other side and came back. I already knew that I had passed and I was just testing him."

"When did you leave the ICU?"

"Until Friday afternoon when they shipped me up here to pass."

"Why did they take you out of ICU? Were you medically stable?"

"No. I put up with the respirator down my throat as long as I could. Friday morning I told them to take it out. I just wanted to pass in peace and be with my husband and family. They were calling me."

"What happened when they removed the respirator?"

"I couldn't breath very well, but I was content and ready for my next journey."

"Then what happened?"

"Some wimpy nurse called my son about noon, told him that my oxygen level was dropping fast and that the doctor wanted him to come to the hospital and convince me to allow them to put that tube back down my throat."

"Did he?"

"Of course! He was here in ten minutes!"

"Did he try to convince you to allow them to reinsert the respirator?"

"He pleaded, begged and even cried, but I had made up my mind."

"Then what?"

"I thought that you were in a big hurry to leave?"

"It's only six forty-eight. I have lots of time before my shift is over. If you need more time I'll stay longer. But I have to get out of here by seven fifteen."

"I appreciate your concern, but why seven fifteen?"

"Hold it! Don't tell her!" Emma cautioned. *"She'll fret about the children and will try to stop it. It has to happen and we can't interfere with it."*

"I've got a breakfast date at Denny's with a couple of horny nurses."

"Now that's important to a virile man like you. I'll make it fast."

"Thank you. Please continue. You left off in the ICU when your son pleaded with you to allow the respirator to be reinserted."

"You have excellent short-term recall. He conferred with the supervising nurse and she told him that my oxygen level would slowly fall until I lost consciousness and passed. My son and the nurse came back into my room and he asked me what I wanted. I told him to stop all treatment and let me pass to be with Ed because he was calling me. Ed was my husband."

"I know."

"My son wanted to be certain that I knew what I was doing and he made me repeat it three times in front of the nurse.

Afterwards he spoke to my doctor over the telephone and confirmed my choice with him. It was difficult for my son to do and he told me that I was stronger than he was because he would not have been able to make that decision for me."

"Then what?"

"He waited for an hour to see what was going to happen before he called my daughter and her son to tell them my situation. He felt that it would be better if I passed without them seeing me that way."

"But you didn't."

"I tried very hard and he told me that it was okay, but I couldn't go even though Ed and my family were calling me to join them."

"Why couldn't you? You were certainly beyond recovery at that point."

"I wanted to see my other grandchildren and make peace with them before I passed."

"Did you?"

"Yes. My son called his son in Fort Lauderdale and his daughter in Orlando and they came to see me on Saturday. My grandson drove to Sebastian on Sunday, picked up his son and brought him to see me on that morning. After that I was satisfied and could relax. I was ready to go."

"That was Sunday and this is Tuesday morning. Why did it take you so long to get to this point?"

"I don't know. On Saturday my son asked me if there was anything special that I wanted to eat and for some dumb reason I told him mashed potatoes and gravy. He ran out of my room and drove to a Kentucky Fried Chicken store and brought back a small container of mashed potatoes and gravy. It tasted really good."

"Did it perk you up?"

"Yes, for a few minutes and I thought that I was going to snap back. Actually, I did have a comeback on Monday morning, but the doctor knew that it was an only endorphin rush. You do know what that is don't you?"

"Yes, I've seen it many times and it is a common occurrence in people who are in the final stages of passing. The mind can't accept that the body is dying and it sends out a rush of endorphins to stimulate the muscles into action as a final act. Many family members interpret that flurry of activity as a sign that the person is recovering, or in some cases even a miracle, but the medical staff knows what is going on."

"I woke up my son up singing, '*I am woman, hear me roar*' and he thought that he was hallucinating. He flew out the room, dashed up to the nurses' station and asked the supervising nurse to call my doctor and re-start my medications. She called my doctor , but he knew what was happening."

"Did your doctor show up?"

"Yes, and he asked my son if he believed in miracles."

"What did your son say in response?"

"No. He told the doctor that he suspected that I'd experienced an endorphin rush."

"The doctor made small talk, and even ordered breakfast for me, but he knew that the time was near."

"Wow! What a great story. So, are you ready to go now?"

"I think so. Aren't you about to get off? It's six fifty-two."

"Do you mind?"

"No. Doctor, you go ahead. I want to spend some quality time with my son before I go."

"*Get going you big lug!*" Emma shrieked in my head. "*You did your job and she's ready.*"

"*Aren't you going to come in and show her the way?*" I thought as I dropped Betty's hand, stood up and turned to leave her room. "*She needs you now!*"

"*No she doesn't.*"

"*Why not?*"

"*I'll explain it to you later. Get out of there and meet me on the elevator. The new shift is coming on duty and they don't need us around to get in their way.*"

I shook my head and slumped my tired shoulders as I schlepped out of Betty's room. I paused at the doorway and looked back at her. Her head was resting on her pillow, her eyes were closed and she had a smile on her ashen face.

"*My job is over, but where's Emma?*" I mumbled as I stumbled out of the room into the hall. It was 6:54 A.M.

Chapter
21

"*What is life? What is death? Exactly where does each one begin and ultimately end?*" I muttered under my breath as I shook my head and slumped against the wall outside of Betty McElroy's room. "*No one ever said that life is easy, but neither is the finality of death. Does mortal life end at the time of death, or does a new life begin when another one comes to an end?*"

"Doctor, are you okay?" Emma's voice cooed in my brain. "*You've had long night and it's time to call it quits and head for the elevator.*"

"Emma! Where were you? I needed your help with that last patient!"

"*I was around, but you didn't need me. You did just fine.*"

"Do you mind if I just stand here for awhile and catch my breath?"

"*Take your time. I have to catch up on paperwork. I'll wait for you by the elevator.*"

Then, just as suddenly as her voice had appeared in my head and interrupted my thoughts, it was gone and I was left alone in the hallway to ponder the night's events. I had been a witness to the passing of several human beings from different walks of life into an unknown dimension.

I was trained as a physician to examine each patient carefully, develop a diagnosis and a prognosis, and prescribe treatment to alleviate their symptoms, or cure their illness. This past evening I was not permitted to do either and only served as a facilitator for the patient's thoughts before Emma appeared and scooped their spirit out of the open window into an unknown dimension. The nurses ignored me, but that's not uncommon because they have their specific functions to perform based on the doctor's evaluation and ultimate orders for treatment. It is not the nurses' role to evaluate a patient's condition, or prescribe treatment, but only to carry out the physician's orders.

I allowed my tired eyes to close and began to silently muse.

"Why did I even bother to make rounds tonight? Emma had already made her decisions about which patients were going to pass tonight and which ones were to live. Why did she constantly interrupt me during my evaluations? Wait a minute! I didn't make any physical evaluations tonight! I only talked to patients about themselves and their lives before Emma showed up and scooped their spirit away!" Then suddenly my tired mind shifted gears.

"What about the innocent kids on that school bus that's going to get whacked by a truck at the Rivergate Plaza at seven twenty-four this morning? I should get down to Port St. Lucie Boulevard and try to warn them, but Emma warned me not to get involved with changing predetermined events. I should try to stop the accident from occurring! If I don't prevent it, and several children are severely injured, the Emergency Room will fill up, followed by the Intensive Care Unit and the Third Floor. Emma will have to free up space up here so that the ER to ICU pipeline flows freely."

I shook my head in a futile attempt to come back to reality, but my eyes wouldn't open and my mind began tossing things around like a load of wet clothes in a hot air dryer.

"I know that I was hallucinating tonight. I didn't have enough rest and the lack of food caused a tinge of hyperglycemia. I should have gone downstairs to the lobby and picked up a candy bar out of the vending machine when I felt the hallucinations coming. I'm a trained physician and I should know that spirits are a figment of a person's imagination caused by a lack of oxygen, or sugar, in the blood resulting in the erratic firing of neural synapses in the starved brain cells. That's what causes dying patients to often imagine that they see a bright light at the end of a dark tunnel. I'll be okay after I've had some coffee and breakfast. When my blood sugar level comes back up to a normal level the hallucinations will disappear."

I forced my eyes open, shook my head to get the cobwebs out and stood up straight. My shoulders ached and there was a crick in my neck. I turned right towards the elevator at the end of the hall, took one step and heard voices behind me.

"Goodbye doctor," rang out a chorus of mixed male and female voices.

I turned to my left and looked down the hall. There stood each patient that I had met that night.

"Thank you for listening to us tonight," their voices echoed, as one as they faded to nothing.

I shook my head and headed for the elevator.

Chapter
22

The round, white-faced clock mounted on the wall read 6:59 when I finally made it past the nurses' station and headed for the elevator. I reached for the 'down' button and the brushed aluminum elevator doors opened as if by cue.

"*Hello doctor, we've been expecting you,*" Emma's soft voice cooed in my ears. I clearly heard her voice, but I couldn't see her!

"Emma! Is that you?" I stammered. "Where are you."

"*We're right here in the elevator.*" Emma's body formed in front of me! She was gorgeous with glowing green eyes and long black hair that flowed down her back and across her ample breasts.

"What do you mean we? Who's with you?"

"Lois of course. We finished our rounds fifteen minutes ago."

"*I told you that I'd be coming back to bug you,*" Lois' voice echoed in my ear but I couldn't see her. "*I figured that you could use some help on your rounds.*"

"We've been bugging the nurses by opening and closing the elevator door while we were waiting for you to finish with that last patient," chimed in Emma. "They think that the elevator's broken."

"What's going on?" I stammered. "Is someone playing mind games with me?"

"Hush down," Emma ordered. "The nurses already suspect that we're in here. Don't blow your cover."

"Emma!" I shouted. What are you talking about? I don't have any cover."

"Yes you do. You've been one of us for almost a week?"

"What do you mean one of us?"

"I mean like Lois and me. Don't you remember falling down with chest pains in Room 306 on Wednesday night? At two seventeen in the morning you grabbed your chest and hit the floor like a ton of bricks. The duty nurse didn't find you until almost three o'clock when she checked in on the patient. You were long gone and no one opened the window for you. Your spirit is trapped in here just like Lois and me."

"Do you mean that I'm not real? I'm a spirit?"

"You're real. Didn't you just make your rounds just like you have for the past twenty-two years?"

"Yes, but I failed. Almost all of the patients died."

"They didn't die. They passed on to a better place. They're free now. You helped them on their way. That's your new job and you'll be making rounds with Lois and me every night until the end of Eternity. I'll show both of you the ropes tomorrow night. I have a copy of the updated 'Spirit Handbook' in my locker for each you."

"So, that's why you didn't open Lois' window? You wanted her to stay here with you."

"No, she wanted to stay here with you. She's had a big crush on you for years. Lois, come out here so he can see you and tell him."

"*I'm too embarrassed,*" whispered a soft female voice from the back corner of the elevator car.

"Lois? Is that really you?"

"Yes doctor. It's me." Lois' body slowly materialized into

view in the corner of the elevator car. She was wearing her white nurses' uniform and smiling like an imp. "I thought you could use some help and I'm used to working this floor. Do you mind?"

"Of course not! Can the other nurses see you?"

"No, they can't see her, me or you either," Emma responded. "We can see each other because spirits can see other spirits, but only if the other spirit wants to be seen."

"Didn't you recognize me when I was talking to you outside of Room 309?" Lois whispered.

"That was you? I tried not to look."

"Yes. You said that you were dictating a patient's notes into a digital recorder in your sleeve, but I knew that you were talking to Emma. Was it really true when you told me that your zipper was stuck? I would've helped you fix it. I've done it before when we were messing around in the supply room."

"Are you two lovebirds going to stand there all night cooing at each other?" Emma barked. "Look at those gawking nurses over there. They think that the elevator door is stuck open. Get in here so we can get down to the cafeteria. Don't you want a hot cup of coffee?"

"Can they hear us talking?" I inquired as I stepped into the elevator car.

"They know that we're here, but they can't hear our words. They just kind of feel them. It feels like a warm summer breeze blowing across their face."

"Emma!" Lois' voice hit a high pitch. "I think they're getting suspicious!"

"Push the 'down' button and let's get out of here!" Emma responded. "I've got to file my report with the Spirit Resources Department by seven-thirty, or I'll get my butt chewed out."

"I'm a spirit! I don't have any hands! How can I push a button?"

"Try it. You might be surprised," Emma responded.

Lois pushed the 'down' button, the brushed aluminum doors closed and Emma, Lois and I were on our way down.

"Emma, what about Betty McElroy?"

"What about her?"

"She was waiting for you to come in to see her and help her

pass. She's ready to go."

"That's old news. Betty passed at four-seventeen this morning."

"*I hope this elevator's fast!*" I thought to myself. "*I have to make it to Rivergate Shopping Plaza on Port St. Lucie Boulevard before seven twenty-four! The paramedics are going to need my help!*"

Chapter
23

"Jeanne! Did you see that?" Asked Debbie, the young, wide-eyed rookie Phillipino nurse who graduated from nursing school only two weeks earlier. This was Debbie's first real nursing job.

"Did I see what?" Responded Jeanne the veteran RN duty nurse.

"The elevator door opened up and stayed open for almost five minutes. No one was on it! What made it stay open all by itself?"

"It was only Emma. She leaves about this time every morning. She must have forgotten something and left the elevator door open."

"Who's Emma? Am I missing something here?"

"You might be. How long have you worked on this floor?"

"I started last Wednesday night. Why?"

"Wasn't that the night the graveyard shift doctor had a heart attack and died in Room 306? He'd been making night rounds in the hospital for twenty-two years. Lois Halfast, the nurse that passed away in Room 306 tonight also worked on this floor for years. She had a big crush on him and everyone knew it."

"Yes. I remember. I was the one who found him on the floor when I went in to give my patient their meds at three o'clock," Debbie eagerly responded. "He was gone when I found him."

"Did you open the window for him?"

"No. Why should I?"

"Didn't anyone explain the *Spirit Chaser* to you at orientation?"

"No! What are you talking about?"

"Emma."

"Who's Emma?"

"She's the *Spirit Chaser*. She comes in at exactly one-seventeen every morning."

"What are you talking about?"

"Emma was a terminal cancer patient who died at one-seventeen in Room 306 three years ago. A new nurse was on duty that night and no one told her that she was supposed to open the window and let Emma's spirit out when she passed away."

"What! Are you nuts?"

"Every nurse with more than a month's experience in any hospital knows that you have to open the window for a dying patient at the time of death to allow the person's spirit to escape the hospital. If you don't let the spirit out they will be trapped in here and forced to roam the floor for Eternity."

"You're pulling my leg! Is this something like a snipe hunt for the new kid on the block? I'm not completely naïve."

"Didn't you see the elevator doors open up at one-seventeen and no one got off of it?"

"Yes. But so what?"

"That's the exact time Emma died. Ever since the night Emma died in Room 306 the elevator opens up at one-seventeen and no one gets out. We're certain that it's Emma's spirit. It's trapped here."

"Wow! That's really eerie. Have you ever seen her spirit?"

"No. But we can feel her presence when she comes by the nurses' station. It feels like a warm summer breeze blowing across your face."

"Why does she come back?"

"She's trying to help the spirits of dying patients escape. She opens the windows for them."

"Wow!"

"We know when a patient is about to pass because we hear voices coming from their room. When we go in to check on them the patient has passed and their window is always open. That's a sign that Emma was there."

"That happened to me twice tonight!" Debbie offered. "I heard voices and I thought that I was going nuts!"

"What room numbers?"

"Room 301 about two-thirty this morning. Marilyn was with me! The patient was Linda Brown, the gal with cervical cancer. She was only thirty-five years old and her parents didn't come to see her before she died. I clearly heard both a man's and a woman's voice. Is Emma a man?"

"Of course not! Does Emma sound like a man's name to you?"

"No. When we went in to check on Linda she was gone and there was no one in her room."

"Was her window open?"

"Yes. It was."

"Did you open it?"

"No."

"Marilyn, did you hear voices come out of Room 301?"

"Yes, but I hear voices all the time. It's normal for me."

"That happened to me tonight too," piped in Hazel, the blonde pony-tailed nurse, as she looked up from her computer terminal. "It's kind of eerie isn't it?"

"What happened to you?" Responded Jeanne, the veteran RN duty nurse.

"I heard two voices over the patient monitoring system intercom from one of my patient's rooms and when I got down there to check on her she had passed and the window was wide open. There wasn't anyone else in the room."

"Hazel!" Jeanne exclaimed. "Come over here and talk to me!"

"Why?" Hazel asked as she glanced up from her computer terminal. "I'm trying to finish up my patients' reports."

"Now!"

"Okay," Hazel responded as she slid her chair over to the nurses' station to continue the animated conversation. "Mary Beth was with me. I told her that it was Emma and she thought that I was pulling her leg."

"What room and what patient was it?"

"Room 304 about three-thirty. It was Kara, the little girl with brain cancer."

"I think we have a problem," responded the duty nurse.

"What kind of problem?" Asked Debbie the rookie nurse.

"The doctor who died in Room 306 last week made night rounds on this floor for over twenty years. I think that he's back. Emma must have a partner."

"When I found him on the floor last Wednesday night the window wasn't open," Debbie responded.

"That's it! Emma does have a partner! She needed a doctor to make rounds with her and he was the perfect choice! Did anyone see a male doctor on the floor making rounds tonight?"

"There was a young guy up here about eleven o'clock or so," Debbie quipped. "He made a quick stop in each patient's room and left about midnight."

"That's it!" Jeanne exclaimed.

"What?" Debbie hesitantly answered. "What did I do now?"

"What was the other room number where you heard voices?"

"Room 306. That was the nurse who worked here for so many years."

"What time did you hear the voices?"

"About four-fifteen. Hazel was there with me. We both heard it. I thought it was the TV set, but it wasn't turned on. Hazel told me that it was Emma, but I didn't believe her."

"Hazel, did you hear voices coming out of Room 306 when you were down there with Debbie?"

"I heard a man's voice too."

"Folks, I think that the good doctor is back," responded the duty nurse.

"What do you mean by that?" Asked Debbie, the still somewhat naïve rookie nurse.

"I think that Emma held back the doctor's spirit last week and tonight the two of them got together and gathered Lois into their fold. And I'm glad for all of them."

"What do you mean you're glad? I'm afraid of ghosts!"

"Don't worry Deb. They aren't ghosts and they won't hurt you. They're lost spirits and they're here to help our patients find peace within themselves before they pass. I like it."

"Jeanne, I should have told you that something strange happened when Marilyn and I went to check on the patient in Room 308 about six o'clock," offered Cathy as she looked up from making notes in a patient's file from her position at the front of the nurses' station.

"What do you mean by strange?"

"I distinctly heard a man's voice over the patient monitoring intercom system and again just before we entered her room. When we got in her room she had already passed, the window was wide open and there was no one else in the room."

"Who was in that room?"

"A cute thirteen year-old girl named Libby McGraw. She had retinal cancer that metastasized into her brain. The surgeons removed both of her eyes the day before she died."

"I heard a man's voice too just before we entered the room," Marilyn offered from her seat at a computer terminal located a few feet away. "I didn't tell you because I thought I was hearing things. I hear voices in my head all the time."

"You didn't stick around very long after hearing those voices did you?" Cathy chuckled. "You left me to do all the clean up work. You're a wimp."

"I had to pee and you wouldn't let me use the patient's bathroom!" Marilyn offered in her defense.

"That's because I had to pee too and we both couldn't use the toilet at the same time. After you left I went in the bathroom to pee and there was something really strange about the toilet."

"What was that," the duty nurse asked. "Was the toilet seat too cold for your fat butt?"

"No! The toilet seat was up," Cathy quipped as she smiled. "But I put it down."

"Gals, let's call it a night and let the day shift take over. I expect to see all of you here tonight no later than a quarter to seven so you can be briefed before going on duty."

"Jeanne, do you need me to fill in again tonight?" Marilyn asked. "I'd really like to come back if you can use me and I can use the extra money."

"I think so. I have a feeling that we're going to be swamped tonight. I just heard several sirens heading in the direction of Port St. Lucie Boulevard."

"There's an elementary school down there," Cathy meekly offered. "My kids go to school there and they ride the school bus every morning."

"It's probably an accident on the turnpike or I-95. I wouldn't worry about it," the duty nurse responded with a frown. "Marilyn, plan on being here tonight. We can use the extra help."

"What about Emma and her buddies?" Hazel questioned. "Will they be here too? It's creepy to be working with ghosts."

"Watch the elevator at two-seventeen. If it opens, and no one gets on or off, you'll know that Emma's back. Hopefully Lois and the doctor will be with her. We can use their help too."

"Does anybody know anything about the patient in Room 310? I heard voices in there just before shift change?"

"That's Betty McElroy. She passed at four-seventeen this morning and the funeral home was called to pick her up. I haven't seen them yet."

"What about her son?"

"He stayed with her all night and went home about a half hour after she passed. She's alone now. There's no one in her room."

"Didn't he say that he's an author?"

"Yes. He came out here about two-thirty this morning and asked me for a piece of paper. When he left about a quarter to five he told me that he had outlined a book about his experiences on this floor."

"Do you think that he'll really write a book about us?"

"He already has the title."

"Really? What is it?"

"*Spirit Chaser.*"

Epilogue

Why did I write *SPIRIT CHASER?*

I wasn't given a choice and I didn't really write this book. I listened carefully to what Emma, the nightshift nurses and my mother told me. Somehow I managed to put it down on paper

The last night my mother was alive and gasping for breath as the pneumonia filled up her lungs with body fluids I tried to write on my laptop in her room. The room was dark except for the small amount of light emitted from the computer screen. She lifted the washcloth off her eyes, sat up and asked me to turn it off because the light bothered her eyes. I did as she asked and after she fell asleep I went out to the nurses' station.

At 1:17 A.M. the elevator door opened and it was empty! I felt a warm breeze softly waft across my face and then it was gone. I innocently asked one of the nurses, "Did you see the elevator door open and that no one got off?"

"Don't worry about it," she tersely replied. "That's Emma. She stops by every night about this time to make her rounds and check on our patients."

"Who's Emma?" I stupidly asked. "I didn't see anyone get off the elevator."

"Emma's the spirit of a woman who passed away in Room 306 three years ago," she responded with a tongue-in-cheek smile. "A new nurse was on the floor that night and didn't know that she was supposed to open the window to let Emma's spirit escape when she passed. Emma's trapped here for Eternity."

I knew that I was being set up, but I played along and smiled as I stupidly responded. "And monsters live under the patients' beds don't they?"

She pounced! "As a matter of fact, a blue, furry monster lives in the closet in one of the rooms on the fourth floor, but we don't have any monsters or ghosts on this floor."

"What about Emma?" I quipped, "Isn't she a ghost?"

"No! She's a spirit and there's a very big difference. Emma's not here to scare anyone. She's a spirit guide that assists our dying patients pass on to the next dimension."

I tried again. "Have you ever seen Emma?"

"Of course not!" The nurse was quick on the uptake. "Human beings can't see spirits."

"Then how do you know that she's really here?"

"Did you feel a warm breeze on your face when the elevator door opened?"

"Yes. So what?"

"That's Emma's way of telling us that she's here." The nurse went back to filling out a patient's report. "Are you satisfied now?" She quipped without looking up from her paperwork.

"Have you ever seen her?" Now I was being redundant.

"I already told you that she's a spirit and humans can't see spirits, but our patients can."

"Patients are human! How do you know they can see her?"

"We hear her talking to them in their room."

"Right!" I took the bait and she set the hook!

"When we check on the patient we find that they've passed away and their window is always open. Emma converses with the patient's spirit, not the patient." Check mate!

That's why I wrote *SPIRIT CHASER* and I sincerely hope that you enjoyed it.

Paul McElroy

Acknowledgements

Life is a long, arduous journey towards eventual death filled with joy, pain, laugher, tears, fear, contentment and hopefully some amount of self-fulfillment.

However, it is not until we reach the end of that terrible journey that we can find true peace. The best we can hope for is that our final weeks, days, hours and minutes will be filled with visits from our loved ones and free from physical pain and mental anguish over the unknown journey that lies ahead.

I am fortunate because I experienced those things first-hand. I am not afraid of the final journey and am looking forward to whatever may lay ahead because I have been there. I attempted to share my experiences with you through the pages of this tale

Many people including doctors, nurses, clergy, patients and their family members, personal friends and business associates all shared in the development of this unique series of ten personal, heart-wrenching adventures. I thank each of them from the bottom of my heart.

Paul McElroy is president of Charter Industry Services, Inc. headquartered in Stuart, Florida. The company specializes in conducting professional maritime training courses. He founded *Charter Industry* a trade journal for professionals in the marine charter industry in 1985. He has extensive writing experience in magazines and newspapers with more than 200 published articles to his credit.

Captain McElroy received his first United States Coast Guard license in 1983 and operated a sport fishing charter business in the Chicago area for several years. He currently holds a Merchant Marine Officer's MASTER - Near Coastal license He served in the United States Air Force, spent a two-year tour in the Far East and specialized in electronics. He speaks Japanese and Spanish.

Paul received his Bachelor of Science Degree in Business Administration from Florida State University. Prior to joining the maritime industry he was an executive in the headquarters of a major telecommunications corporation. He lives in south Florida with his wife Michi, is a member of the Mystery Writers of America and the National Association of Maritime Educators.

SPIRIT CHASER is Paul's fifth novel.

Contact him at: www.TreasureCoastMysteries.com